Frank and Fearless

By
Horatio Alger

CHAPTER I.

JASPER'S VICTORY.

A dozen boys were playing ball in a field adjoining the boarding-school of Dr. Pericles Benton, in the town of Walltham, a hundred and twenty-five miles northeast of the city of New York. These boys varied in age from thirteen to seventeen. In another part of the field a few younger boys were amusing themselves. All these boys were boarding-scholars connected with the school.

The ball had been knocked to a distance by the batter, and it was the duty of Nicholas Thorne, one of the oldest boys, to ran after it. But he thought of an easier way.

"Cameron, run for that ball!" he cried, addressing one of the smaller boys outside the game.

"I don't want to," said little Cameron.

"Did you hear what I said?" demanded Thorne, imperiously.

"Yes."

"Then you'd better go if you know what's best for yourself," said the bully, frowning.

"I ain't in the game," said Cameron. "Why should I get the ball?"

"Because I say so!" retorted the tyrant.

"Run after it yourself, Thorne," said a lad named Davies. "It's your business, not Cameron's."

"It's his business, because I ordered him to do it," said Thorne, flushed and angry. "Do you think I will allow him to bully me?"

"The boot's on the other leg," said Davies, dryly. "Run after the ball, and don't keep the game waiting."

"That's so," said half a dozen voices. "Let Cameron alone."

"I won't let him alone," said Thorne, who had by this time worked himself into a towering passion. "I'll give him the worst flogging he ever had, if he doesn't obey me!"

So saying, he advanced toward Cameron in a menacing manner.

Thorne was the acknowledged bully of the school. He was a big, hulking fellow, with a heavy figure and a repulsive face, and small ferret eyes, emitting a cold and baleful light. He was more than a match for any of his fellow-pupils, and availed himself of his superior physical strength to abuse and browbeat the smaller boys. Knowing his strength he was not afraid of interference, and usually carried his point. If Cameron had not been particularly occupied playing marbles with a boy of his own age he would not have ventured to object to obey the despot. When he saw Thorne advancing toward him with a cruel light in his eyes he became frightened, and said, hurriedly:

"Don't pound me, Thorne, I'll go."

"Yes," said Thorne, between his teeth, "you'll go; but you ought to have done so at first. I'll give you something to remind you to be more prompt next time."

"Don't hit me, Thorne!" pleaded the little boy, with tears in his eyes. "I'm going."

"Shame, Thorne!" exclaimed Davies.

Thorne glared at Davies wrathfully.

"Take care how you talk," he said, "or it'll be your turn next!"

Davies was two inches shorter than Thorne, and by no means his equal. So, honestly indignant as he was, he didn't venture to say any more.

Little Cameron turned to run, despairing of help, and Thorne started to pursue him. Of course there was no chance of the smaller boy's escape, or would not have been, but for an unexpected incident.

"Stop!" was heard, in a clear, commanding voice.

Thorne turned in surprise. What boy (for it was a boy's voice) had dared to command him to atop?

He wasn't long in doubt.

Jasper Kent, a new scholar, who had only arrived the day before, advanced intrepidly to the rescue of the little victim. He was an inch shorter than Thorne, of a slight, elegant build, with a clear complexion and a bright, attractive face that would have been pronounced handsome by anyone. Judging from outward appearances, no one would have thought him the equal of Thorne in strength.

When Nicholas Thorne's eye lighted on his antagonist his lip turned in scorn and he paused.

"You're the new boy, I believe?" he said.

"Yes."

"I thought so. If you had been here longer you would know better than to interfere with me."

This was spoken with the utmost arrogance.

"You appear to consider yourself master here," said Jasper, quietly.

"I am master here," returned Nicholas, in the same tone.

"And you claim the right of ordering around smaller boys?"

"I do."

"And of beating them if they dare to disobey your majesty's commands, I suppose?" continued Jasper, with sarcasm.

"Yes, I do. Have you anything to say about it?" exclaimed the young despot, in a swaggering manner.

"Yes, I have," was the quiet answer.

"What have you got to say, I should like to know?"

"That I won't allow it," said Jasper.

"You won't allow it?" exclaimed Thorne, bursting into a brutal laugh. "And who are you, young poppinjay?"

"My name is Jasper Kent, at your service."

"Then, Mr. Jasper Kent, I beg leave to suggest that you mind your own business."

"I generally do," said Jasper, coolly; "but that advice comes with a bad grace from you."

"Why does it?"

"Because you are not attending to your business."

"What is my business?" demanded Thorne, angrily.

"To go after that ball."

"It's Cameron's business. I ordered him to go after it."

"And I order him not to go for it," said Jasper, resolutely, but without excitement.

Thorne answered with an oath.

"I've a great mind to send you for it," he exclaimed, his small eyes glaring at his opponent.

"It's one thing to order, and another to secure obedience," said Jasper.

"Your turn will come," growled Thorne, "but just at present I've got Cameron's case to dispose of. Cameron, go for that ball!"

The little boy started, but his purpose was interrupted. Jasper Kent hurried forward and placed his hand kindly on his shoulder.

"Don't go, Cameron," he said. "I'll protect you."

Cameron stopped, but looked apprehensively at Thorne. He evidently doubted the power of his young protector.

Thorne was now thoroughly exasperated. His authority was openly defied. He rushed at Jasper, intending to overwhelm him by the suddenness and momentum of his attack. But Jasper was prepared for him. He turned swiftly aside and planted a blow on Thorne's right ear which sent him staggering to the earth.

The bully was astonished, but rallied. Almost foaming at the mouth with rage, he sprang to his feet and renewed the attack. He attempted to throw his arms round the waist of Jasper and throw him. Had his tactics been successful, probably Jasper would have been borne to the earth by the superior weight of his opponent. But here, again, he was prepared. He stepped back and received Thorne with a blow on his breast, so firmly planted that he staggered again.

By this time he had lost all control of himself and was thoroughly under the dominion of passion. He "pitched into" Jasper, trying to get in a blow wherever he could, and in so doing exposed himself to the skilful blows of his slighter foe, who had some knowledge of boxing, while Thorne had none whatever.

Finally Thorne was stretched on his back, not immediately to rise.

"Have you had enough?" asked Jasper, bending over him.

"I'll kill you!" shrieked Thorne.

"Wail till you are able," said Jasper.

Thorne struggled to rise. Jasper held him down forcibly.

"You will stay there till you promise to let Cameron alone," he said.

"I won't promise!"

"Then you'll stay where you are."

But at that moment a small boy came across the field from the school.

"Thorne is wanted," he said. "There's a lady to see him."

"You can rise, then," said Jasper.

Thorne rose sullenly, and without a word strode toward the large, square building, with an extended wing, which was used for the boarding-school.

Little Cameron seized Jasper's hand and kissed it.

"How brave you are!" he said. "How much I thank you!"

"Oh, it's nothing," said Jasper, modestly. "You just send for me when you're in trouble, Cameron. I won't let him hurt you."

CHAPTER II.

STRANGE NEWS.

Entering the house, Thorne reported at the doctor's study. His flushed appearance attracted the teacher's attention.

"What's the matter, Thorne?" he asked.

"The new boy pitched into me and I licked him," said Thorne.

But his sullen manner was so unlike that of a victor that the doctor shrewdly suspected that his statement was not wholly correct.

"What was the quarrel about?" he asked.

"We were playing ball," said Thorne, evasively.

"I will inquire into it. At present you are wanted in the parlor."

So Thorne left the presence of the principal and entered the opposite room. A lady, seated on a sofa, arose quickly, and advanced to meet him. She kissed the boy's cheek, to which he submitted without manifesting any responsive feeling.

"How long it is since I saw you, Nicholas, my dear boy!" she said.

"It's only about six months," said Nicholas, stolidly.

"And are not six months long for a mother to be separated from her only child?" said the lady, tenderly.

"It doesn't seem so long," said Nicholas.

The lady looked pained, but she proceeded:

"How you have grown!"

"Yes, I've grown," said Nicholas, showing a little pleasure now. "I think I shall be a large man."

"Like your father. And how are you improving in your studies, Nicholas?"

"Oh! I'm doing well enough," said the boy, indifferently, for Nicholas Thorne's taste for study was very moderate. "Did you bring me any money, mother?"

"You have your regular allowance, Nicholas."

"It isn't enough. What's a dollar a week?"

"It is a good deal for me to pay," said his mother. "Remember, I have to pay your school bills, and my means are but small."

"A dollar a week is very small for a boy of my age," grumbled Thorne. "Why, some of the little boys get more; and there's that new boy, Jasper Kent, gets five dollars, so they say."

The lady betrayed strong interest at the sound of his name.

"I forgot," she said. "So Jasper Kent has arrived, has he?"

"What, mother, do you know him?" demanded Thorne, surprised in turn.

"Yea, I know him. What do you think of him?"

"Think of him? I hate him!" said Thorne, fiercely.

"Why?"

"He tries to bully me."

"And you permit it? Why, you are larger than he."

"Yes, but he knows how to fight."

"How do you know?"

"I had a fight with him this morning," said Nicholas.

"Did he come off best?" asked the lady.

"No," answered Nicholas, with hesitation. "That is, we were only half through the fight when a boy ran up and said you had come. So we had to stop."

"Humph! That is strange," said the lady, in a low voice, more to herself than to her son, "this sudden antagonism."

"What do you know about Kent?" demanded Nicholas, his curiosity aroused.

"Perhaps I may as well tell you," said his mother, thoughtfully, "but I wish you to keep the matter secret from him."

"You won't catch me telling him anything, except that he is a scoundrel!" muttered Nicholas.

"Then sit down by me, and I will tell you much that you do not know, but ought now to hear. Is the door shut?"

"Yes."

"Go and see. It is important that no one should overhear us."

Nicholas complied with her request.

"It's shut fast enough," he said. "Now what have you got to tell me?"

"To begin with, do you know where I get the money I pay for your schooling and clothes?"

"My father left you some money, didn't he?"

"He left me a small property which rents for two hundred dollars a year."

"You pay three hundred a year for me, don't you?"

"For your school bills, yes. Besides, I give you an allowance and buy your clothes."

"How do you do it?" asked Nicholas, in surprise. "Have you sold the house?"

"No. If I should do that, there would soon be nothing left. That was the problem I had to solve three years ago, when your father died."

"What did you do?"

"I felt that the property must not be touched, save the income. I saw that it was necessary for me to exert myself, or I should be unable to educate you as I desired. I had a good education, and I determined to avail myself of it. I therefore went to a teacher's agency in New York and set forth my desire to obtain the position of governess in some family in the country."

"You a governess!"

"Why not? It was the only way I could think of that would yield me an income. After waiting a few weeks I succeeded. A wealthy gentleman, living in a country town of moderate size, saw my testimonials, was pleased with them, and engaged me to superintend the education of an orphan niece resident in his family. He offered me a fair salary—enough, added to the rent which I received from the property left me by your father, to justify me in putting you at this boarding-school. That was three years ago."

"Why didn't you tell me all this before, mother?"

"It would have done no good. I preferred that you should think of me as possessing an independent property. I felt that it would enable you the better to hold up your head among your school-fellows, as they could know nothing of your antecedents."

"Does Dr. Benton know this?" asked Nicholas, quickly.

"No; he only knows that I am a widow, He supposes that I have sufficient means."

"I am glad of that."

"Would it make any difference with him?"

"I don't know. Any way, I'd rather he wouldn't know it."

Nicholas Thorne sat by his mother's side thoughtful. He was disappointed to think that his mother's means were so limited, since it curtailed his future expectations. The thought of that mother working patiently to defray his expenses at school made comparatively little impression. He was essentially selfish, and, so long as his wants were provided for, he cared little who labored for him.

"You don't ask the name of the man who employs me," said his mother.

Nicholas looked up.

"I suppose it is nobody I ever heard of," he said.

"No, you never heard of him, but you know some one connected with him."

"What do you mean?" asked the boy, his curiosity aroused.

"The gentleman who employs me is father of one of your schoolmates."

"Father of one of my school-mates?"

"Yes."

"Who is it? Why don't you tell me, mother?"

"You have spoken of him to me this morning. It is Jasper Kent."

"You work for Jasper Kent's father!" exclaimed Nicholas in unbounded astonishment. "Does he know it?"

"Yes, he knows that I am, or have been, governess in his father's family. But he knows nothing of my connection with you."

"If he knew, he'd taunt me with my mother's being obliged to work for a living," said Thorne.

"I don't think he would. At any rate, the time is coming very soon when he will have no advantage over you."

"How do you make that out, mother?"

"Listen, and keep secret what I tell you. Next week I become his father's wife."

"You marry Jasper Kent's father!"

"Yes; I shall be Jasper's step-mother."

"Is old Kent rich?" asked Nicholas, eagerly.

His mother nodded.

"Yes, he is rich; that is, for the country. He is in poor health, too," she added, significantly.

"Good!" said Nicholas, with satisfaction. "You know how to play your cards, mother."

The mother smiled.

"My days of dependence are drawing to an end," she said. "Some time I can do better for you than I am doing now."

CHAPTER III.

JASPER RECOGNIZES THE VISITOR.

"Will the old man do anything for me after he marries you, mother?" asked Nicholas, who never failed to look out for his own interests.

"He doesn't know you are in existence, Nicholas."

"Did you never speak to him of me?"

"No; I didn't dare to tell him."

"Why not?"

"It might prevent his marrying me."

"It seems to me," grumbled Nicholas, "you only thought of yourself. You didn't care what became of me."

"That is unjust, Nicholas. You must see that it is. Once we are married I shall have more control of money, and if Mr. Kent dies I shall be entitled to a third of his property."

"I wish he'd leave you the whole, and cut off that upstart Jasper," said Nicholas, frowning.

"There is not much chance of that. He thinks everything of Jasper. However, I don't think he'll live long, and I shall induce him, if possible, to name me as Jasper's guardian."

"That would be a good job for you, mother—not so good for Jasper, I'm thinking."

"You are right, Nicholas. Did you say you disliked him?"

"Yes, I hate him."

"So do I," said his mother in a low tone, but one of intense energy.

"Why?" asked Thorne, in some curiosity.

"I'll tell you. From my entrance into his father's family he has never treated me with any cordiality. Evidently he didn't like me. I think, indeed, he mistrusted me, though I never gave occasion for any suspicions. If he should learn now that I am to marry his father, he would move heaven and earth to prevent the marriage."

"Has he been home much since you were in the house?"

"No; he was at school elsewhere, and was only at home during his vacations."

"How did he come to be sent here to this school? Did you advise it?"

"No; I was opposed to it, but Mr. Kent was recommended by a friend to send his son here. I did not venture to say much, lest I should be asked how I came to know anything of the school. I was afraid you and he would meet, and he would learn the connections between us."

"I suppose you'll own up after the wedding, won't you?"

"I think not at once, Nicholas."

"Why not?"

"Remember what I told you, that Mr. Kent is in poor health. He may not live six months. We can keep the matter secret for that time, can't we, Nicholas?"

"If you were only sure he would die in that time."

"He has heart disease, and is liable to die at any time."

"You want him to make his will first, and leave you guardian?"

"Of course."

"After that you wouldn't mourn very much for his loss?"

"No; I don't pretend to care for him."

"He thinks you do, eh, mother?"

"Of course."

"Oh, you're a deep one, you are," said Nicholas, winking in a way to indicate his shrewd insight into his mother's motives.

"I have to be, Nicholas. There's no getting on in this world without it. But I think I shall have to leave you now."

"Then you don't mean to invite me to the wedding, mother?"

"It will be a private ceremony."

"Will Jasper be invited?"

"His father was anxious to have him at home. Indeed, I have had a great deal of trouble to prevent his sending for him, but at length I have succeeded. I know too well the danger. The boy has a great influence over his father, whose mind is weakened with his body, and I should be afraid that the match would be broken off even at the last moment if the boy got wind of our plan."

"How mad Jasper will be when he hears of it!" said Thorne, laughing with malicious enjoyment. "I wish I could tell him."

"Don't breathe a word of it, Nicholas," said his mother, in evident alarm.

"Oh, I'll keep the secret. But it won't do any harm when it's all over, will it?"

"Say nothing till I authorize it."

"Well, I won't, then, if I can help it. But I say, mother, the old gentleman will come down handsomely when you're married. You ought to raise my allowance to two dollars a week."

"I will if I can afford it," said his mother. "But I must leave you now, Nicholas. I shall have about time to go to the station and meet the next train."

"Shan't I go with you?"

"I should like your company, my dear boy, but we must be prudent. We might meet Jasper Kent."

"That's so. Well, good-bye."

"Good-bye, Nicholas," and his mother pressed her lips upon the cheek of her son.

He tolerated the kiss, but did not return it. His heart was not very impressible, and he cared for no one except himself.

"I won't stop to see Dr. Benton," she said, at parting. "You may tell him that I was in haste."

"All right."

Mrs. Thorne emerged from the parlor and from the house. She was tall and erect in figure, and walked rapidly. Her face was concealed by a thick veil, but, for the information of the reader it may be described as narrow and long, with small eyes, like those of Nicholas, and thin, tightly-compressed lips. She was not a woman to yield to misfortune or give way to sentimental sorrow. She looked rather like one who knew how to face fortune and defy it. It was not a pleasant face, but it was decidedly a strong one.

The grounds of the school were extensive, and the house stood back two or three hundred yards from the street. A long avenue led from the house to the main thoroughfare.

Mrs. Thorne looked hurriedly about her as she went out on her way.

"I shouldn't like to meet Jasper Kent," she said to herself. "It might lead to unpleasant questions and suspicions on his part, and I don't want anything to happen before I am married."

It seemed likely that she would escape the encounter which she dreaded. Had there been no interruption or delay she would have done so; but it was not so to be. She met Dr. Benton in front of the house, and was compelled to stop and speak to him.

"You find Nicholas well?" he said, politely.

"Oh, yes, doctor," she answered, softly. "I have no anxiety on that subject, as long as he is under your care. I know that he cannot fail to do well."

We all like flattery, and the learned principal was not proof against it.

"Ahem! Mrs. Thorne," he said, pompously, "we try to do our duty by the young people intrusted to our charge. We do not limit our endeavors to their mental culture, but strive to promote their physical well-being also."

"And you succeed remarkably well, Dr. Benton. But you must excuse my leaving you abruptly. I wish to catch the next train."

"I hope we shall see you again soon, madam," said the doctor, politely.

"I shall endeavor to call again before many weeks, Dr. Benton. Good-morning."

"Good-morning, madam."

Mrs. Thorne adjusted her veil and swiftly resumed her course. Her heart gave a bound when, just outside the gate, she espied the well-known figure of Jasper Kent.

"I hope he won't recognize me," she thought

But she forgot her peculiar gait, and the quick, rapid step, which were likely to identify her in the eyes of anyone who had seen her often. Jasper Kent's attention was drawn to her, and he observed these peculiarities.

"By Jove!" he said to himself, "she walks just like the governess."

Still, having no reason to suspect the presence of Miss Thorne, as he called her, at the school, he would have thought the resemblance only accidental, but for a whiff of wind which blew the veil aside from her face. That face there was no mistaking.

"Miss Thorne!" he exclaimed, in surprise, advancing to meet her.

She was exceedingly vexed, but it would not do to betray it.

"Jasper!" she said, with a smile. "You didn't expect to see me here?"

"No; did you come to see me? Is my father unwell?" he asked, anxiously.

"Your father is quite well."

"Then—"

"Why have I come? I see that is what you wish to ask. I have not come on your account at all. I came to see a nephew of my own."

"At this school?"

"Yes."

"You must mean Nicholas Thorne."

"Yes; do you know him?"

"A little," said Jasper, with reserve.

"Poor fellow! He has neither father nor mother to look after him, only myself. I am his only relative living."

"I never heard you speak of him before."

"No; I have not cared to intrude my private concerns upon your father or yourself. But I must hurry, or I shall be late at the station. Have you any message to send to your father?"

"Give him my love, and tell him to take care of his health for my sake."

"I hope he will do that for all our sakes," said the lady, with affected warmth. "Good-bye."

"Good-bye."

Jasper Kent looked after her as she walked rapidly away.

"Why is it that I distrust her so much?" he thought to himself. "So she is Thorne's aunt. Well, he is not a relation to be proud of."

"How vexatious that I should meet him," thought Mrs. Thorne. "I ought not to have run the risk of coming. If he tells Nicholas that I have admitted a relationship it may do harm. Once the wedding is over I shall feel more secure."

CHAPTER IV.

THORNE'S REVENGE.

The unexpected communication which Thorne had received from his mother influenced his treatment of Jasper. Under ordinary circumstances he would have resented bitterly the humiliating defeat he had received at the hands of the "new boy." Now, however, he felt sure of ultimate revenge, and was willing to "bide his time."

"Just wait till his father is dead, and mother is his guardian!" he said to himself. "Then, my young gentleman, your pride'll be taken down, see if it ain't!"

His politic forbearance surprised the other boys, who did not understand the secret cause.

"Ain't you goin' to lick that new boy?" asked Tower, a sycophantic follower of Thorne.

"What for?" asked Nicholas.

"Because he licked you the other day."

"Who says he licked me?" demanded the young tyrant, with a frown.

"Why, all the boys say so," stammered Tower.

"Do you say so?" demanded Nicholas, savagely.

"N-no," said Tower, timidly.

"Lucky you don't," said Thorne, significantly. "I'll lick any boy that tells such a lie about me."

Tower was silent.

"The fact is," he continued, in a milder tone, "we were stopped in the middle of the fight. I was called to see a lady visitor. But for that I should have licked him in the end."

"I guess you can lick him," said the young sycophant.

"Of course I can," said Nicholas, loftily.

"Are you going to try it?"

"Why should I? I haven't anything against him. We came out even. What's the use of bearing malice?"

Tower was astonished to hear such sentiments from Thorne. It did not sound at all like him. He was about the last boy who would be singled out for forbearance or forgiveness of injuries. So the younger boy concluded that his leader was afraid of Jasper. But here he did him wrong. Thorne had learned to respect his adversary's strength and skill, but he would have hazarded a second encounter but for the prudential reasons already suggested. For the present he thought it best to keep quiet.

Jasper also had made a discovery, though, as we know, the information he had received was not correct. He supposed Thorne to be a nephew of his father's governess, whereas she was his mother.

"Does Thorne know this?" he asked himself.

He could not feel quite satisfied on this point, nor could he determine precisely how far his feelings were affected by this discovery. He felt a dislike toward Thorne on account of his tyrannical disposition and ill-treatment of younger boys. He cherished a dislike for the governess, the cause of which he could not as well define. Now, it appeared that these two were allied to each other. I beg to say that Jasper was too sensible and gentlemanly to dislike the governess simply because she was poor. That he knew very well had nothing to do with the substantial worth of a person. But he could not rid himself of the feeling that Miss Thorne's residence in his father's family portended misfortune to the parent whom he loved so well.

So a week passed without any new disturbance or outbreak between the two boys. Jasper had been on the lookout, fearing that Thorne would take some opportunity to wreak vengeance on young Cameron when he was not present. But his fears were gradually allayed. Thorne seemed usually peaceable—so much so that his school-mates, who knew him well, thought he had turned over a new leaf, and speculated as to what had produced the change. But neither boys nor men change suddenly and completely, though policy and self-interest may for a time lead them to suppress the manifestation of their characteristic traits.

Nine days after the fight recorded in my first chapter, as Jasper was walking in the school-yard, Davies came up hurriedly.

"Kent," he said, "you're wanted."

"Who wants me?" asked Jasper. "Is it Dr. Benton?"

"No, the doctor's absent."

"Who wants me, then?"

"Little Cameron."

"What! is Thorne at him again?" asked Jasper, stopping short and looking toward the house.

"Yes, Thorne's at his old business, bullying him. He took the opportunity when he thought you were out of hearing."

"I must stop it," said Jasper. "Where are they?"

"In the back yard."

"I suppose I shall have to fight him again," said Kent, regretfully.

"You needn't be afraid to try it. You are a match for him."

"I think I am. That is not my reason."

"What then?"

"I don't like fighting—it's brutal. Besides, I have another reason, which I don't care to mention."

By this time they had reached the scene of the difficulty, Little Cameron was half-crying, and Thorne stood over him with upraised arm.

"Do as I tell you, you little blackguard!" he was just saying, when a voice he well knew was heard, calm and resolute:

"Thorne, are you bullying that boy again?"

Nicholas turned and saw his old antagonist. He was sorry to see him, but he could not well withdraw now.

"It's none of your business," he answered, sullenly.

"I shall make it my business to protect the weak," said Jasper, quietly.

"You may need to protect yourself," sneered Thorne.

"If necessary, I feel competent to do so. Cameron, come here."

"Don't you go!" said Thorne, menacingly.

The little boy looked in terror from one to the other. Evidently he dreaded that the immediate result of his obeying Kent would be to precipitate a blow from the bully.

Jasper saw the little boy's quandary, and he quickly advanced to the rescue. Throwing one arm protectingly round Cameron's waist, he regarded Nicholas firmly.

"Well," he said, "what do you propose to do?"

Thorne had had time to think. He hated Jasper worse than ever, but he knew that our hero did not care for blows. Moreover, he was likely to give back better than he received. There was another way of wounding him, which prudence would have led him to hold in reserve. But he was too angry to be prudent. Moreover, he had had a note two days before from his mother, from which he learned that the wedding was to be solemnized on that very day. Probably at that moment his mother was Mrs. Kent.

"I won't fight," he said, with an unpleasant smile, "seeing we're relations."

"Relations!" repeated Jasper, with a look of surprise and inquiry. "I don't know what you mean."

"You'll know soon enough," said Thorne, mockingly.

A suspicion of the truth entered Jasper's mind. He turned pale, and said:

"Will you step aside with me, Thorne, and tell me what you mean!"

"If you like," said Thorne, indifferently.

"Now," said Jasper, when they had withdrawn a few rods from the other boys.

"It appears you haven't heard the news," said Thorne, with malicious enjoyment. "Your father has married my mother. That makes us step-brothers, doesn't it?"

"My father married again!" said Jasper, recoiling as if he had received a blow.

"Yes. Strange you wasn't invited to the wedding, isn't it?"

An hour later Jasper, having obtained special permission from Dr. Benton, was on his way home, sick with apprehension lest this threatened misfortune should prove real.

CHAPTER V.

JASPER'S RETURN HOME.

His father married again, and he left in ignorance of his intention! Jasper felt hurt that his father, for whom he cherished so deep and warm an affection, should have taken such a step without apprising him of it in advance. If he was to marry, certainly his only son ought to have been present at the wedding.

"But it isn't father's fault," he thought, bitterly. "It's the fault of Miss Thorne. She is more artful and designing even than I thought. She has married my father for his wealth and position, and she was afraid I would dissuade him from such a step."

It was certainly a bitter thought that he must look upon this woman as his step-mother—that she was to take the place of the mother whom he tenderly remembered, though six years had passed since she left him. But, after all, was it true? Might it not be the case that Thorne, who evidently disliked him, had fabricated the story in order to annoy him? There was a gleam of comfort in this, and he felt that he would willingly run the risk of being laughed at for having started on a "wild-goose chase" if only his fears could be relieved. But, after all, there was the possibility—nay, the probability, considering what he knew of Miss Thorne—that Thorne's story was all true.

The cars stopped for a brief minute at the depot in Morton, Jasper's destination, and he jumped out. He looked eagerly about him to see if there was anyone of whom he could ask information. To his joy he caught sight of John, a serving-man in his father's employ.

"Halloo, John!" he cried, "give me a hand with my valise!"

"Why, Master Jasper!" returned John, in evident surprise, "I didn't know you were coming home."

"I am not expected," said Jasper. "I came at a moment's notice."

"You're too late for the wedding, Master Jasper."

"For the wedding!" repeated Jasper, his heart sinking at this confirmation of his worst fears.

"Yes; didn't you know of it?"

"I heard something, but not much. Tell me about it. When did it take place?"

"At ten o'clock this morning."

"At the house?"

"No; your father and the governess walked over to the church, and were married private like. There was nobody invited, but we were all surprised that you didn't come to it."

"I knew nothing about it," said Jasper, sadly.

"It was Miss Thorne's doings, then—leastways, I must say Mrs. Kent's, now."

"I know it, John. My father would not have treated me that way. How long has it been going on—the—"

"The courtship? Well, that was all on the side of Miss Thorne, I'm thinkin'. She wheedled your father into marrying her."

"I wish I had been here."

"Poor man! he felt too weak to resist, and he did it only because she teased him. I can take my oath of that."

"It is infamous!" said Jasper. "Have they gone away?"

"No; they ain't goin', I've heard. Your father don't feel able to travel, and the governess—I mean your step-mother—she don't care much. They're at home now."

"Then I will go up. I suppose they will be surprised to see me."

"Yes, they will, but your father'll be glad. He sets the world by you, Master Jasper."

"I believe he does, John," said Jasper. "I wish I could have saved him from this misfortune."

"It's too late now entirely."

"You are right. I don't know but it might be best for me to turn round and go back again to school without going to the house at all; but I must face this thing, and see for myself. If you've got nothing else to do, John, you may carry my valise."

"I'll do it, Master Jasper, directly. You go up to the house, and I'll be there in a jiffy."

So Jasper walked thoughtfully and sadly homeward.

We must precede him.

In a sunny sitting-room on the second-floor sat Jasper Kent's father in a luxurious arm-chair. He was barely fifty, but evidently a chronic invalid. His constitution had been undermined years before by a residence of several years in Central America, where he had acquired a fortune, but paid a costly price therefor in the loss of his health.

For years he had done no business other than to take care of his property, which was amply sufficient to enable him to live luxuriously. Yet he did not find the time hanging heavily upon his hands. Of a studious taste, he had surrounded himself with books and pictures. He received regularly a New York daily paper, and the leading magazines and reviews, and barring his ill-health, and occasional seasons of pain, passed his time in a placid and agreeable manner. Circumstances, perhaps, had fostered a disposition to indolence, and made it more difficult to resist the artful schemes of Miss Thorne, whom he had admitted into the house as governess of his little niece, Florence Grantley, but who had from the first cherished the ambitious design of making herself mistress of the establishment.

It is needless to recapitulate the steps she took in this direction. It is enough to chronicle her ultimate success.

We introduce the newly-married pair, as they sit conversing in the pleasant sitting-room already referred to.

"I think Jasper ought to be at once informed of our marriage," said Mr. Kent.

"There is no need of haste, in my opinion, my dear," said Mrs. Kent.

"Indeed, he ought to have been present at the ceremony. I am afraid the poor boy will feel hurt that I should have left him wholly in the dark."

Mrs. Kent's lip curled. Evidently she had no particular feeling for the "poor boy."

"Lay the whole blame upon me, Mr. Kent," she said. "It was I who advised it, and I am willing to take the responsibility."

"I know you advised it, my dear," said Mr. Kent, to whom this phrase was yet new; "but I could not understand why."

"I will explain, and I think you will consider my explanation a good one. It would have taken Jasper's attention from his studies, and it might have been some time before he would have been able to resume them to advantage."

"That may be, but still on an occasion of this kind—"

"If the ceremony had not been so private—wholly out of regard to your health —of course he should have been recalled. As it is, it is better on all accounts not to disturb him. Did I tell you that I saw him last week?"

"Saw Jasper?"

"Yes."

"Was he here? Why did I not see him?" asked Mr. Kent, in surprise.

"It was not here that I saw him—it was at his school."

"At his school! How came you to go there?" inquired her husband in still greater surprise.

"I will tell you, though I have hitherto kept it a secret, as a matter of my own. Now, since I am your wife, it is only proper that I should acquaint you with it. I have a nephew at the same school."

"You have a nephew at Dr. Benton's boarding-school?"

"Yes," answered Mrs. Kent, lowering her voice to a compassionate inflection. "Poor boy! he has neither father nor mother! He is entirely dependent upon me. Out of my salary I have paid his expenses ever since I entered your employ."

"That was generous and kind of you," said her husband, approvingly. "What is the boy's name?"

"Nicholas Thorne."

"Your brother's son, I suppose?" said Mr. Kent.

"Ye—es," she replied, hesitatingly.

"What is his age?"

"Sixteen. He is about the same age as Jasper. Do I venture too much in asking you to become his friend?"

Mrs. Kent modulated her voice, as she well knew how to do, to counterfeit warm and tender feeling, as she proffered this request. Her nature was feline, and she knew how to conceal her claws.

"You may rely upon my co-operation, my dear," said Mr. Kent, kindly, "in your noble task."

There was a latent gleam of triumph in Mrs. Kent's eyes as she heard this promise, which transferred to her husband a burden which had long been a drain upon her own slender purse. She had dreaded the effect of this announcement upon her husband, and finally, as we have seen, thought it best to change the relationship and call Nicholas her nephew, and not her son. So that difficulty was well surmounted, and the effect had been to impress Mr. Kent with a sense of her generous and unselfish devotion.

But her exultation was short-lived. A bustle was heard outside. An instant later the door was thrown open, and Jasper entered the room, flushed and excited.

CHAPTER VI.

THE STEP-MOTHER.

"Jasper!" exclaimed his father, in surprise, but showing pleasure, nevertheless, at his son's unexpected presence.

The boy went straight up to his father, passing within two feet of his father's wife, but without even looking at her.

"Father!" he burst forth, impulsively, "is it true?"

"Is what true?" asked his father, embarrassed, for he guessed what Jasper meant.

"Are you married—to her?" pointing to Mrs. Kent, who looked indignant at the reference.

"Yes, Jasper," answered his father, nervously. "Shake hands with your—with Mrs. Kent."

He was about to say "your mother," but something in his memory, perhaps something in his son's face, led him to change the expression.

Jasper did not apparently heed the suggestion. Instead, he said, reproachfully:

"Why was it, father, that you left me in ignorance of your intention?"

"She thought it best," said his father, in an apologetic tone.

Mrs. Kent spoke for the first time.

"Yes, Jasper, we thought it would only interrupt your studies."

Jasper could not help a slight sneer, as he answered:

"You were very considerate, madam; but it seems to me that such an important event in my father's life would justify an interruption."

Mrs. Kent repressed her real feelings of anger and vexation, and answered mildly, and with an affectation of good humor:

"I don't know but you are right, Jasper, and we were wrong. At any rate, since you have come it is a pity you were not here earlier, so that you could have been present at the ceremony. It was quite private, as your father can tell you."

"Yes, Jasper, there were no invitations issued," said his father.

"I wish that I had come earlier," said Jasper, slowly.

"At any rate, now that you are here," said Mrs. Kent, with well-feigned cordiality, for it was politic to keep on good terms with Jasper, since he was his father's favorite, "you will stay a day or two."

"You forget, madam, the interruption to my studies," said Jasper.

"I should like to wring the boy's neck," thought Mrs. Kent, her eyes contracting slightly, but she answered, amiably: "I am afraid I have thought too much of that already. Let me make amends by welcoming you, and asking you to stay as long as you can."

Mr. Kent nodded approvingly at these words of his wife.

"I ought not to complain," said Jasper, "since you treated me no worse than you did your own son."

"Nicholas has betrayed my secret!" thought Mrs. Kent, turning pale.

"What are you talking about, Jasper?" demanded Mr. Kent, surprised. "My wife has no son."

"Jasper means my nephew," explained Mrs. Kent, recovering her assurance.

"He said you were his mother," said Jasper.

"Yes," said Mrs. Kent, with admirable composure, "the poor boy has always looked upon me as a mother, though such is not our relationship. Indeed, I may say, orphan as he is, I have been a mother to him."

"And it is very much to your credit, my dear," said Mr. Kent, kindly. "We must have him here on a visit. As Jasper's schoolmate, and your nephew, he shall be doubly welcome."

"You are very kind, Mr. Kent," said his wife, in a tone which might well be mistaken for that of grateful emotion. "It will, indeed, be a treat to my poor Nicholas to come here, even for a day."

"He must spend his next vacation here, eh, Jasper? It will be pleasant for you to have a boy of your own age here."

"Do as you like, father," said Jasper, who didn't care to say how distasteful the proposition was to him, or to explain the nature of the relations between Nicholas and himself.

Mrs. Kent looked at him sharply as he spoke, and understood better how he felt. But, as he did not openly object, she was satisfied. It was what she had wished to bring about, and she felt pleased that the proposal had come from Mr. Kent, and that Jasper had not spoken against it.

"I will go and order your room to be made ready for you, Jasper," she said.

"You had better write to Dr. Benton that you will stay with us a day or two."

So saying, she left the room, and Jasper was left alone with his father.

"Don't you like this marriage, Jasper?" asked his father, anxiously, seeing that his son looked sober.

"No, father," answered Jasper, frankly. "I have not yet got over the shock of the first news."

"You think I ought to have told you about it."

"You are not accustomed to keep secrets from me, father."

"I did it for the best, Jasper; I wanted to tell you, but she—Mrs. Kent—thought it best not."

"I am afraid, father," said Jasper, sadly, "it will not be the only time that she is destined to come between us."

"No, Jasper," answered his father, with more energy than was usual with him, "that shall not be. I am sure she would not wish it, and I know I wouldn't permit it. I hope, my dear boy, that you will become reconciled to the new state of things."

"One thing would reconcile me to it," said Jasper.

"What is it?"

"To be assured that it would promote your happiness."

"I feel sure that it will," said Mr. Kent, but he did not speak very confidently.

"If it be so, it is all I ask. But tell me, father, did you marry for love?"

Mr. Kent hesitated.

"I am too old for that, Jasper," he answered, pleasantly. "The fact is, I need a nurse and Miss Thorne needed a home; and, in fact, without pretending to any sentimental reason, we concluded that it would be the best thing under the circumstances."

"Was she very much surprised when you made the proposal, father?" asked Jasper, significantly.

"No, I can't say she was," answered his father, embarrassed.

"It is as I thought," Jasper said to himself; "she inveigled my father into the marriage."

He said aloud:

"Well, father, I heartily hope it will be for your happiness; and now let us talk about something else. Shall I tell you about the school?"

"Yes, Jasper."

So Jasper gossiped about school matters in a way that interested his father, and the two forgot for a time that a new tie had been formed that might possibly make a difference between them.

Meanwhile Mrs. Kent, instead of giving directions about Jasper's room, opened her writing-desk and wrote a hurried note to Nicholas. In this she said:

"Remember, Nicholas, you are to pass for my nephew. Why were you so imprudent as to tell Jasper I was your mother? I have explained that you regard me as a mother, though really my nephew. You must give the same explanation. Jasper is at home now, not very well pleased to find that he has a step-mother. But it is done, and he will find it can't be undone. Be prudent, follow my directions implicitly, and you will find it to your account.

"Your devoted aunt,

"MATILDA THORNE KENT.

"P.S.—I have told Mr. Kent about you, and he authorizes me to invite you here to spend the next vacation."

CHAPTER VII.

NEW RELATIONS.

Jasper remained till the next afternoon. His father urged him to stay longer, and his step-mother, with apparent cordiality, seconded the invitation; but Jasper felt that the charm of home was gone. The new wife had stepped in between his father and himself. He felt sure that the marriage had not been of his father's seeking. To him it was no object. To the former governess it was a matter of importance, since it secured her a permanent home and position, and a share of Mr. Kent's property.

There was an old servant in the family, a trusty maid, who had been in it before Jasper was born. With her he could speak confidentially.

"Tell me, Margaret," he asked, "how came my father to marry Miss Thorne?"

Margaret went to the door and looked out cautiously, then closed it.

"I don't want her to hear what I say," she commenced, when convinced that they were in no danger of listeners, "but it's my belief she asked your father to marry her."

"Do you really believe that, Margaret?"

"Yes, I do, Master Jasper. She's that bold she wouldn't mind it, not a bit. Only she'd do it sly-like. I know just how she'd do it. She'd tell him how she hadn't got a home, and must go out into the wide world, and get him to pity her.

Then, you know, he'd got used to seeing her round, and a sick man don't like changes."

"Why couldn't she stay as governess to Florence?"

"According to her father's will Florence is to pass the next four years in the family of his sister, and she—that's her aunt—has a governess for her own children that'll do for Florence, too. So there wasn't no need of Miss Thorne staying here any longer. Your father asked her to stay a while, till she could find another place. It's my belief she didn't try, being bent on staying here as the mistress. At any rate, she told your father she couldn't get a place, and he offered her the one she wanted, that of his wife."

"How do you like her, Margaret?" asked Jasper, thoughtfully.

"Me like her! That's what I never did. She's like a cat—soft-spoken enough when she has her own way, but she's got claws, and you may depend she'll show 'em. I hope she won't do anything to harm you, Master Jasper."

"Me!" said Jasper, with the bold confidence of a boy, laughing at the thought. "What can Mrs. Kent—a woman—do to injure me? I'll risk that, Margaret. It's of my father I'm thinking. Will she treat him well?"

"I think she will, for it's her object to, Master Jasper. She's married him for money, you know."

"I don't mind her benefiting by my father's property, if she will make him comfortable during his life."

"I think she will; she's too sly, and knows her own interest too well not to."

"I'm glad you think that, Margaret. I shall feel better about it."

"Then you don't think you can stay, Jasper?" said Mrs. Kent, softly, when he announced his determination.

"No, madam, I think I ought to be getting back to school."

"Perhaps you are right. We shall miss you."

"Yes, Jasper, we shall miss you," said his father.

"I will write you often, father. If you are not feeling well at any time, write and let me know."

"I will do so, Jasper," said his step-mother, promptly; "but I shall have better news to write. Your father shall have the best of care."

"Thank you, madam. If you can contribute to his comfort, you will place me under obligations to you."

"As a wife, it will be my duty as well as my pleasure to do so," said Mrs. Kent.

Jasper bowed. The suggestion of the relationship always fell unpleasantly on his ears.

The carriage came round to take Jasper to the depot. His father and step-mother looked out of the front windows, and saw him off.

"He is a noble, warm-hearted boy," said his father, warmly.

"Yes," said Mrs. Kent, assenting, because it was expected.

"Manly and high-spirited, too!" added his father, in a tone full of affectionate admiration.

"I'd like to break his spirit!" thought Mrs. Kent, spitefully. "Some time I may have the chance." Of course she didn't venture to say this. She only inquired, "Were you like him at his age, Mr. Kent?"

Mr. Kent smiled.

"I won't flatter myself so far," he answered. "Jasper is an improvement on the parent stock. I see in him more manliness and self-reliance than I possessed at his age."

"May it not be parental partiality?" asked Mrs. Kent, who by no means enjoyed hearing Jasper's praises.

"No, I don't think so."

"You must let me believe that it is your modesty then. Jasper may be a fine boy, but he will do well if he grows up as good a man as you."

"Now you flatter me, my dear," said Mr. Kent, smiling. "You have too good an opinion of me."

"I don't know about that," said Mrs. Kent to herself. "I think you are an addle-headed old fool, but I won't say so."

Aloud she said, with a smile: "My marrying you is a proof of my good opinion, Mr. Kent."

"Thank you," said her husband, politely.

He was not a suspicious man—far from it—but even he knew that his wife only married him for a home and an establishment. But he never let his mind dwell on such things, and he quietly permitted his wife's assertion to go uncontradicted.

Meanwhile Jasper Kent had returned to his boarding-school. There was one who awaited his return with mingled curiosity and exultation.

This was Nicholas Thorne.

He had received his mother's letter, from which he learned, first, that her plan had succeeded, and she was now the wife of a rich man, and, secondly, that his own relationship to her must be changed in the eyes of the world.

"I suppose mother knows what is best," he said to himself. "So I'm to be her nephew, am I? Well, it's all one to me, as long as I fare the better for her good fortune."

For the moment it occurred to him that his mother might intend to throw him off—in a measure—but he quickly laid it aside. Bad as his mother was, she was yet devoted to him, and in so far was superior to him, for he cared for himself first and for no one second. The thought originated in his own base selfishness, and was laid aside only because he had received too many proof's of his mother's affection to doubt her.

When he heard that Jasper had got back he took pains to meet him.

"Well, Kent," he said, with a show of intimacy which Jasper found very disagreeable, "what news from home?"

Jasper was about to reply abruptly, when it occurred to him that, after all, Nicholas had an interest in the matter.

"I suppose you mean to ask if your mother is well?" he said, eyeing Jasper keenly.

But Nicholas was on his guard. His mother's letter had cautioned him.

"No, I don't," he answered, impudently. "She is your mother, not mine."

"My mother!" exclaimed Jasper, coloring.

"Yes, she's your father's wife, isn't she?" said Thorne, with a leer.

"Yes, but I acknowledge no such relationship as you suggest."

"She's your step-mother, whatever you say."

"I shall never call her so. You told me before I went that she was your mother."

"I have always called her so, because I have known no other," said Thorne, composedly. "She is really my aunt."

"It must be true, then," thought Jasper. "However, it is of little importance to me what the relationship may be."

"I suppose this match makes us relations," said Thorne, smiling disagreeably.

"I don't see that it does," said Jasper, coldly.

"You'd rather it wouldn't, I suppose," sneered Thorne, provoked.

"I don't know you well enough to desire so close a connection," said Jasper, in the same cold tone.

"We shall know each other well enough some time," said Thorne, with something of menace in his tone.

Jasper turned on his heel and walked away.

CHAPTER VIII.
SUDDEN DEATH.

Two months later there was a vacation for a week. Nicholas expected to spend this with his mother, but for some reason Mrs. Kent gave him no invitation. Probably she thought that Nicholas, though a paragon in her eyes, was not likely to win favor in the eyes of Mr. Kent. His rough, brutal disposition would have repelled the sick man, who had become gentle in his enforced seclusion.

Thorne was disappointed, but his disappointment was softened by a timely remittance of ten dollars from his mother, which he spent partly in surreptitious games of billiards, partly in overloading his stomach with pastry and nearly making himself sick.

Jasper spent the week at home. His company was the source of great comfort and joy to his father, and this repaid him for the intrusion of his step-mother.

She treated him with politeness and apparent cordiality, but once or twice, when he chanced to look up unexpectedly, he detected her eyes fixed upon him with a glance that seemed to express detestation. On these occasions her expression changed instantly, and she addressed him in a soft, friendly voice.

All this puzzled him.

"Does she hate me or not?" he asked himself. "I certainly don't like her. Still, I shall force myself to treat her politely as long as she treats my father well."

His father seldom spoke of his wife to his son, but sometimes Jasper noticed that he breathed a sigh of relief when she left the room, as if her presence had been a restraint upon him.

He didn't like to ask his father any question directly as to the relations between them. He hoped that at least they did not add to his father's discomfort.

At the end of the week Jasper was about to return to school.

"How long before you have another vacation, Jasper?" asked his father, wistfully.

"Eleven weeks, father."

"It seems a long time, Jasper."

"I can come home during that time."

"To my mind such interruptions of study are bad for a boy," said Mrs. Kent.

"Perhaps they are," assented Mr. Kent, reluctantly.

"I won't let them be an interruption, father," said Jasper. "If you want me to come home, I will."

"I hope, Jasper, you will understand my motive for speaking," said Mrs. Kent, softly. "I should really be glad to see you, but sometimes we have to sacrifice our own inclinations—don't we, Mr. Kent?"

"Yes, my dear," said Mr. Kent, listlessly.

And he turned his eyes once more to Jasper, who had his overcoat on and was waiting for the carriage to convey him to the depot.

"Do you feel as well as usual, father?" asked Jasper, anxiously.

"Yes, I don't know but I do; perhaps a little more languid, but that is not unusual."

"Well, good-bye, father. If you want to see me at any time, write a line, and I'll come at once."

"Thank you, my dear boy. Don't overwork yourself at school."

There was a slight smile on Mrs. Kent's thin lips. Jasper noticed and mentally resented it. But the time had come for leave-taking, and he hurried away.

Six weeks passed. Jasper heard from home that his father was about the same, and this assurance relieved him of anxiety. Still, he made up his mind that he would spend the next Sunday at home. He would go on Saturday morning and come back on Monday morning, and he knew that his father would enjoy even this brief visit. But he was destined to go home quicker.

On Thursday afternoon a boy came up to the main entrance of Dr. Benton's school.

"It's the boy from the telegraph office," said Wilder to Jasper.

"I wonder whether he's got a message for the doctor or one of us boys?" said Jasper, not suspecting that it was for himself.

"I'll ask," said Wilder. "Here, you, boy! who's your telegram for?"

"For Jasper Kent," said the boy. "Will you call him?"

"I am he," said Jasper, hurrying forward, with pale face and beating heart, for a telegram always inspires fear.

"Then here it is. Just sign the book," said the boy.

Jasper scrawled his name hurriedly and tore open the envelope.

These were the brief words of the dispatch:

"Come home, for the Lord's sake, Master Jasper. Your father's dying.

"MARGARET BOWER."

The paper swam before Jasper's eyes.

"What is it, Jasper—bad news?" asked Wilder; but Jasper did not wait to answer. He rushed to Dr. Benton's office, got his permission to go home, packed his valise, and in five minutes was on his way to the depot.

He was just in time for the afternoon train. At seven o'clock in the evening he entered the avenue that led to his father's house. Throwing open the front door, he met Margaret in the hall.

"I'm glad you're here, Master Jasper," said the faithful handmaiden, heartily.

"Is it too late?"

"I hope not; indeed, I hope not."

Jasper waited for no more, but rushed up stairs and into his father's room.

There were two persons there—the step-mother and a man of thirty, with black whiskers and sallow complexion, with whom she was talking earnestly. They, started when Jasper entered, and looked discouraged. Mrs. Kent looked displeased and annoyed.

"How is my father?" exclaimed Jasper, excitedly.

"Hush! He is very low," said Mrs. Kent "You shouldn't have dashed in here so abruptly."

"Is there no hope for him?" asked the boy, sorrowfully.

"No, my young friend," said the man, smoothly. "All has been done that human skill can do, but without avail."

"Are you the doctor?"

"I am."

"Where is Dr. Graham, my father's old doctor?"

"I dismissed him," said his step-mother, "He was not competent to attend so critical a case. This is Dr. Kenyon."

"I never before heard Dr. Graham's skill doubted," said Jasper. "Is my father conscious?"

"No; he is under the influence of morphine. Do not wake him up."

"Was he, then, in great pain?"

"Yes, in great pain."

Quietly Jasper drew near the bedside.

His father lay unconscious, his form rigid, his face thin and betraying marks of weariness and suffering. The tears rose to the eyes of Jasper as he realized that his father was passing away. As he looked on there was a slight convulsive movement; then repose. In that one moment his father had passed on to another world.

The doctor had approached the bedside also, and he, too, saw the movement.

"He is dead!" he announced.

"Dead!" repeated Mrs. Kent, in a voice rather of surprise than of sorrow.

"Yes."

"Well," she said, coolly, "we must all die. We have the satisfaction of knowing that we have done all we could do to preserve his life."

"Certainly, my dear madam; you may comfort yourself by that thought," said the physician.

"Why did you not send for me before?" asked Jasper, turning with moist eyes to his step-mother, "that I might see my father before he died?"

"We could not foresee his sudden death," said Mrs. Kent. "How do you happen to be here this afternoon?"

"Didn't you direct Margaret to telegraph for me?" asked Jasper, surprised.

"Did Margaret take upon herself to telegraph to you?" asked Mrs. Kent, in a tone of displeasure.

"Yes," said Jasper, bitterly. "Did you mean to keep me wholly unacquainted with my father's illness?"

"No; I wrote a line this afternoon, which I should have sent to the office at once."

"When it was too late!"

"Your reproaches are unseemly and uncalled for," said his step-mother, quite coldly.

"I think differently," said Jasper, bitterly. "You should have sent for me as soon as my father got worse than usual."

"In consideration of your grief I will overlook your impertinence," said Mrs. Kent, compressing her thin lips, as she left the room.

The doctor followed her out, and Jasper was left alone with the dead.

He did not realize it, but his father's death was to seriously affect his fortunes.

CHAPTER IX.
A DECLARATION OF WAR.

Half an hour later Jasper left the room where his father lay dead. He did not seek the presence of his step-mother, who, he felt, had done him wrong in keeping from him his father's condition. He went instead to the kitchen, where he found Margaret.

"This is a sad day for you, Master Jasper," said the sympathizing servant.

"It is, indeed, Margaret. I have lost my best friend."

"True for you."

"But for your telegram, I should not have known even now that he was dangerously ill, I thought at first Mrs. Kent asked you to telegraph."

"No, she didn't. I asked her would she send for you, and she told me it was none of my business."

"It was lucky you didn't heed her," said Jasper. "She is a cold, unfeeling woman."

"That she is, Master Jasper," assented Margaret, with emphasis.

"How long has my father been so sick?"

"For a week or more, but he took a sudden turn at the last. I think he got worse after the new doctor came."

"I wanted to ask you about that. Why was Dr. Graham dismissed? He has attended my father for years."

"Shall I tell you what I think, Master Jasper?" said Margaret, stopping short in her work, and looking mysterious.

"Yes."

"Let me whisper it, then. Come nearer, Master Jasper."

Rather surprised at her manner, Jasper obeyed.

"It's my belief," she whispered, "that your step-mother didn't want your father to get well."

Jasper looked horror-struck.

"Are you crazy, Margaret?" he ejaculated.

She nodded her head positively.

"I know what I'm saying," she answered.

"But what can make you believe such a horrible thing?" he asked.

She answered in the same low voice:

"A month ago she got your father to make his will. What there is in it I don't know, but it is likely it suits her. After that she had nothing to gain by his living."

"You don't think she'd—" Jasper hesitated to proceed.

"Poison him? No, I don't. It wasn't needful; but your papa was that delicate, it would be enough if he was not rightly treated, and I don't believe this new doctor did the right thing by him. Dr. Graham and Mrs. Kent never could agree, but she and the new doctor have been as thick as can be. They understand one another, I'll be bound."

Jasper looked shocked, and was silent for a moment.

"I don't like Mrs. Kent," he said, "but, Margaret, I hope you're wrong in this. That any one could wish my dear, gentle father dead I find it hard to believe."

"You haven't seen as much of your step-mother as I have, Master Jasper."

"Heaven grant you are wrong, Margaret! If I thought it were true I should never want to look at the woman again."

"Hush!" said Margaret, suddenly putting her hand on her lip.

Jasper understood her caution, when he saw his step-mother enter the kitchen. She looked from one to the other with a suspicious glance.

"This is a strange place for you, Jasper," said she, in slow, cold accents.

"I don't see why, madam," he answered, in a voice equally cold.

"I find you—a young gentleman—conferring with a servant."

"With a trusted servant, who has been in our family for years. Nothing could be more natural."

"I don't agree with you," said Mrs. Kent, in a chilly tone.

"I am unfortunate in not winning your approbation," said Jasper, not caring to suppress the sarcasm.

"It strikes me you are impertinent," said Mrs. Kent.

She had thrown off the mask. During her husband's life she had taken special pains to be polite to Jasper, though in so doing she did violence to her feelings. There was no more to be gained by it, and she had changed suddenly. Jasper could not help alluding to it.

"How happens it, madam," he said, "that your treatment of me has changed so entirely since my father's death? Brief as the interval is, you have lost no time."

There was hatred in the glance she shot at him.

"I was silent out of regard to your father, who was blind to your faults," she answered. "You must not expect me to be equally blind."

"I don't, madam."

"Do you intend to remain in the kitchen?" demanded Mrs. Kent

"I was questioning Margaret about my father's last days."

"I am the proper one to question."

"Would you have afforded me the information I desired?"

"If the questions you asked were of a proper character."

"Mrs. Kent, I will take you at your word. How does it happen that you dismissed Dr. Graham, my father's old family physician?"

His step-mother hesitated and looked angry, but she replied, after a brief pause:

"He did not understand the case."

"What makes you think so? He certainly ought to understand my father's constitution."

"Perhaps he ought, but he didn't," said Mrs. Kent, sharply.

"You haven't given any reason."

"I have given all I choose. I don't mean to be catechised by a boy."

"Who is this Dr. Kenyon whom you called in afterward?"

"A very skilful physician."

"He looks young."

"He has a high reputation."

"When did he assume charge of my father's case?"

"A week ago."

"And since then he has grown steadily worse."

"Who told you that?" demanded Mrs. Kent, sharply.

"Is it not true?"

"Did Margaret tell you this?"

"I did," said Margaret, quietly.

"I shall remember this," said Mrs. Kent, spitefully.

"I didn't need to ask Margaret," said Jasper, "when my father lies dead after a week's treatment by this skilful physician."

Mrs. Kent was white with anger.

"You ought to know that life and death are in the power of no doctor," she said, for, angry as she was, she saw that it was necessary to reply to what Jasper said. "In sending for Dr. Kenyon I did not much expect that he would cure your father, but I felt that it was my duty to give him this last chance. Unfortunately he was too far gone."

"You thought that matters were as bad as that a week ago, and yet you didn't send for me?" exclaimed Jasper.

"It would have done no good," said she, coldly.

"But it would have been a satisfaction to me to see something of him in his last sickness. Mrs. Kent, you haven't treated me right in this matter."

"Is that the way for a boy to talk to his—elder?"

"Yes, if he says only what is strictly true."

"I shall not continue this conversation," said Mrs. Kent, haughtily, "nor shall I submit to be talked to in this style. It is not for your interest to make me your enemy," she added, significantly.

Jasper was frank and fearless by temperament, and anything in the shape of a menace roused his high spirit.

"That consideration doesn't weigh with me a particle," he said, hastily.

"We will see," she retorted, and with a look of anger she swept from the room.

"Margaret," said Jasper, abruptly, "did you go into my father's sick-chamber at any time?"

"Yes, Master Jasper."

"Did you ever hear my father inquire after me?"

"I heard him say more than once, with a sigh like, that he wished to see you."

"And she wouldn't send for me!" exclaimed Jasper, bitterly.

"She always opposed it, saying it wouldn't do no good, and would only take you off your studies."

"Much she cared for my studies! Margaret, I will never forgive that woman, never!"

"Well, I can't blame you, Master Jasper."

Here Margaret heard her name called in a loud voice, and was forced to obey.

"She wants to separate us," thought Jasper, as he slowly and sadly went up to his own chamber.

CHAPTER X.

NICHOLAS APPEARS UPON THE SCENE.

The funeral was over. Mrs. Kent was considered by those present to display a great deal of fortitude. As she felt no real grief for the death of her husband, this was not remarkable. Jasper looked pale and sorrowful, but gave way to no violent demonstrations of sorrow, though he began to understand that he had not only lost his best friend, but become at the same time exposed to the machinations of a resolute and relentless enemy.

In due time the will was read.

It was very brief, and clear in its provisions.

To Mrs. Kent was left one-third of the estate, real and personal, of which the deceased was possessed, and the balance was willed to his only child and dear son Jasper, of whom his step-mother was left guardian.

When this clause was read Mrs. Kent directed a brief and triumphant glance at Jasper. He met the glance, and understood what it meant. He knew that it boded him no good.

The company assembled gradually dispersed, and Jasper was left alone with his step-mother.

"You see that I am left your guardian," she said.

"Yes," answered Jasper, briefly.

"Perhaps you would have chosen a different one if the choice had been left to you," she continued, with a sneer.

"I should," said Jasper, promptly.

"Well, that is plain language."

"I suppose you expected a plain answer," said the boy, firmly.

"I did not expect a polite one. You appear to forget that I am a lady."

"You are mistaken, madam. I am ready to treat you as well as you treat me. I won't pretend that I like your guardianship, as I fear that we shall not agree."

"If we don't, you will have to yield," said his step-mother.

"I would rather not dispute till it is absolutely necessary," said Jasper. "May I ask whether you desire me to return to school?"

"I have not made up my mind. I may be able to tell you to-morrow."

"Until you make up your mind you expect me to remain at home, I suppose?"

"Yes."

Jasper bowed and turned away. He went down stairs into the hall just as the front door was opened, and the familiar voice of Nicholas Thorne was heard. Jasper stared in some surprise at the intruder, not knowing that he was expected.

"Halloo, Jasper!" said Thorne, boisterously. "How are you?"

"I am well," said Jasper, distantly.

"Where's mother?"

"Your mother? Your aunt, you mean."

"No, I don't. That's all gammon. She's my mother."

"She is!" exclaimed Jasper. "What made you deny it, then?"

"Policy," said Thorne, laughing. "Your father might not have liked it. Now it's all right."

"Did your mother send for you?" asked Jasper.

"Yes, of course she did. This is to be my home now."

Jasper made no comment. What could he say? If Thorne were his step-mother's son, it was only natural that he should live in the house of which she was mistress.

But it seemed to him as if he were being pushed out of his own father's house, and these strangers were coming in to occupy it He felt that it would no longer seem like home to him.

"Well, where's my mother?" asked Thorne.

"She's up stairs. Shall I show you the way?"

"If you're a mind to. I guess I'll know my own way round here pretty soon."

"What a detestable fellow!" thought Jasper. "I am afraid we shall quarrel soon."

He led the way up stairs, and ushered Nicholas into his mother's presence.

This uncouth boy was the one object this selfish woman loved. She uttered an exclamation of delight.

"Welcome home, my dear Nicholas!" she exclaimed, advancing hastily and throwing her arms round his neck.

He received the embrace apathetically, but made no opposition, as at another time he might have done. He felt on good terms with his mother and the whole world, in the face of the brilliant improvement of his prospects.

"Are you well, my dear boy?" asked Mrs. Kent.

"Oh, I'm well enough, mother. This is a splendid old place, isn't it?"

Mrs. Kent laughed at Jasper.

"Yes, it is a fine country-place."

Jasper left the two, and went down stairs.

"Say, mother, how about the will?" asked Thorne. "Is it all right?"

"A third of the estate is left to me."

"Only a third! Does Jasper get the rest?"

"Yes."

"That's a shame. You ought to have had half."

"I shall have control of the whole till Jasper is of age. I am left his guardian."

"That's good, anyhow. You must make him toe the mark, mother."

"I mean to."

"He's always had his own way, and he may give you trouble. He feels high and mighty. I can tell you."

"I shall know how to deal with him," said Mrs. Kent, closing her thin lips resolutely. "He will find me as firm as himself."

"I guess that's so, mother. You'll prove a tough customer."

Mrs. Kent smiled, as if she enjoyed the compliment.

"I'll stand by you, mother. If you have any trouble, just call me in."

"I don't expect to need any help, Nicholas; but I am glad to find I have a brave son, who will stand by his mother."

Certainly no one believed in Nicholas so thoroughly as his mother. To the world generally he was a cowardly bully, rough, brutal, and selfish. In his mother's eyes he was manly and a paragon of youthful virtue. I have already said that Thorne's affection for his mother was far less disinterested, as is very apt to be the case with boys. His intention to benefit by the change of circumstances was shown at once.

"What allowance are you going to give me, mother?" he asked.

"I have not thought, yet, Nicholas."

"Then I want you to think, mother."

"How much do you want?"

"I want as much as Jasper gets."

"You shall receive as much," said his mother, promptly. "Do you know how much he has received?"

"Yes—he has had five dollars a week."

"That's too much."

"It isn't too much for me."

"I shall reduce his allowance to three dollars a week."

"You don't expect me to get along on three dollars?" grumbled Thorne.

"I will give you five."

"And Jasper only three?"

"Yes."

"Won't he be mad!" exclaimed Nicholas, with malicious satisfaction. "What'll you say to him about it?"

"I shall merely announce my decision," said Mrs. Kent, coolly. "I am not bound to assign any reasons."

"Won't there be a precious row!" said Thorne.

"I presume he will complain, but he has not conducted himself toward me in a manner to secure any favors."

"I say, mother, can you give me my first week's allowance in advance? I'm awful hard up."

"Here, my son," said Mrs. Kent, drawing out her pocket-book and placing a five-dollar bill in her son's hand.

"Good for you, mother. When are you going to have supper?"

"In an hour."

"How much property did the old man leave?"

"The estate is probably fully up to one hundred thousand dollars. This place is worth fifteen thousand. The rest is in good interest-paying stocks and bonds."

"And a third belongs to you! I say, mother, you've feathered your nest well. I guess I'll go out and take a look round."

In the rear of the house, in front of the stable, Nicholas caught sight of Jasper.

He smiled maliciously.

"I'll go and tell him about the reduction in his allowance," he said to himself.

CHAPTER XI.

THE OUTBREAK OF HOSTILITIES.

Jasper was quietly thinking over his change of circumstances when he was roused by a rather violent slap on the shoulder.

Turning hastily, he saw that it was Nicholas.

"I say, this is a jolly place, Jasper," said Thorne.

"Yes," said Jasper. "It has been my home as far back as I can remember."

"That's where you have the advantage of me, but after all it doesn't make much difference, as long as it's going to be my home now."

Jasper didn't reply.

"I say, Kent, it seems odd that me and you are brothers," said Thorne, not very grammatically.

"We are not," said Jasper, quickly.

"It's all the same—we've got the same mother."

"You are mistaken," said Jasper, coldly.

"You know what I mean. She's my mother and your step-mother."

"That's very different. Besides, the relationship is so very recent that I find it hard to think of your mother as any relation at all."

"She is, though. I suppose me and you will be a good deal together now."

"I don't know what my future plans will be," said Jasper, not very much elated by this prospect.

"No, I suppose not. Mother'll arrange about them. How much allowance did your father use to give you?"

Jasper thought at first of refusing to reply, but it occurred to him that under the new and strange circumstances it was not an improper question for Nicholas to ask. He therefore decided to reply.

"Five dollars a week," he answered.

"When was it paid?"

"On Saturday."

"See here," said Thorne, drawing from his vest pocket the five-dollar bill his mother had given him.

"What of it?" said Jasper.

"It's my allowance for this week," said Thorne, triumphantly.

"I congratulate you," said Jasper, coldly.

"That's kind in you," returned Thorne, with a sneer, "especially as you are cut down."

"What do you mean?" asked Jasper, hastily.

"Mother says five dollars a week is too much for you. She's going to cut you down to three."

The indignant color came to Jasper's cheek. Was this interloper—this stranger —to be preferred to him in his own father's house? He was not excessively fond of money, and had there been need would not have objected to a reduction of his allowance. But to be deprived of his rights in favor of a fellow like Thorne was intolerable. If Nicholas wished to annoy and anger him, he had succeeded.

"Who told you this?" demanded Jasper, sharply.

"My mother," answered Nicholas, with a gratified smile.

"When?"

"About fifteen minutes ago," replied Thorne, with provoking coolness.

"I don't think she would do anything so outrageous."

"Don't you? You'll find mother's got plenty of grit."

"So have I," said Jasper, his face hardening. "If your mother undertakes to wrong me she will repent it."

"You had better not say that to her," said Thorne, insolently.

"I shall when the proper time comes. My allowance is not due yet. I don't care for the money, but my father knew what it was proper for me to have."

"There's going to be a row," thought Nicholas, with satisfaction. "I'll bet on mother. She'll put down this whipper-snapper."

Jasper turned away, and walked out of the yard.

"Where are you going?" asked Thorne.

"To walk."

"I guess I'll go along, too."

"I would rather go alone."

"You're not very polite."

"Excuse me," said Jasper, with the instinct of a gentleman. "You would find me very poor company. Another time we will walk together."

"Oh, just as you like; I don't want to intrude," said Thorne, sulkily.

They did not meet again till supper. Mrs. Kent presided. On one side sat Nicholas, on the other Jasper. Our hero looked sad. The kind, worn face he was accustomed to see at the head of the table was gone forever. He felt that he was indeed desolate. His appetite was very small, while, on the other hand, Nicholas seemed to be famished. His mother kept plying him with dainties and tidbits, and he appeared to like the treatment amazingly.

"Why don't you eat, Jasper?" asked Thorne with his mouth full.

"I am not hungry."

"I should think your walk might have given you an appetite."

"It doesn't appear to."

"You look awful glum. Is it what I said this afternoon?"

"About what?"

"Your allowance being cut down."

"I wasn't thinking about that particularly. Besides, you are not the one from whom I expect to receive such communications."

"It's all true, though, as you will find. Ain't it, mother?" persisted Nicholas, who was anxious to have the row come off as soon as possible.

Jasper turned his glance upon Mrs. Kent.

"You needn't have introduced the subject, Nicholas," she said, with slight reproof.

"Why not, mother?"

"It isn't a proper subject to introduce at the supper-table."

"You see, Jasper didn't half believe what I told him."

"He may rely upon your statement," said Mrs. Kent.

"Am I to understand that my allowance is reduced to three dollars a week?" asked Jasper, who felt that he had been dragged into the discussion.

"Yes. I consider that three dollars a week is a liberal allowance for a boy of your age."

"My father gave me five."

"Your father acted according to his judgment," said Mrs. Kent, coldly. "On some points I differ from him in judgment. I think that he indulged you too much, probably because you were his only child."

"He was always kind to me," said Jasper. "It was his nature to be kind."

"You will find me kind, too, if you deserve it," said his step-mother. But her tone belied her words.

"Nicholas tells me that his allowance is to be five dollars," said Jasper.

"I conceive that the amount of his allowance has nothing to do with yours," said Mrs. Kent.

"Is it true?" persisted Jasper.

"It is," said Mrs. Kent, with a defiant look, which Jasper interpreted to mean "What are you going to do about it?"

"Why is he to receive five dollars, if I am only to get three?"

"Because I choose."

"You have answered rightly," said Jasper, scornfully. "Even you are unable to defend it on the score of fairness or justice."

Mrs. Kent's thin lips compressed.

"Audacious boy!" she exclaimed, "do you dare to speak to me in this style?"

"I am not aware of any impropriety, madam. I am protesting against your unjust partiality for Nicholas."

"He is my son."

"I am aware of that; but the money out of which the allowance is paid came to you from my father."

"Do you dare to continue your impertinent remarks?" exclaimed his step-mother, pale with rage.

"Madam, I am only stating the truth," said Jasper, sturdily. "You cannot expect me to submit tamely to such an injustice. Had you reduced my allowance and given Nicholas no more I would have let it pass."

"I won't submit to this impertinence!" exclaimed Mrs. Kent, furiously. "Nicholas, will you sit there and see your mother insulted?"

"What do you want me to do, mother?" asked Thorne, not exactly liking the turn matters had taken.

"Put that unmannerly boy out of the room."

"Oh, there ain't any need of that," said Thorne, who knew by experience Jasper's strength.

"Do as I say, or I will give you no allowance at all!" said Mrs. Kent, stamping her foot angrily.

Nicholas unwillingly arose from his seat and approached Jasper.

"You'd better not try it, Thorne," said Jasper, coolly.

"Do you hear that, sir? He has insulted you, too," said Mrs. Kent, in a furious passion.

It was these words, perhaps, that spurred Nicholas to his task. Jasper had now risen, and Thorne threw himself upon him.

But Jasper was prepared. In less time than I have required to tell it, Thorne found himself prostrate on the floor.

"Madam," said Jasper, turning to his step-mother, "I am ready to leave your presence now, but of my own accord."

He left the room. Mrs. Kent was too astonished to speak. She had felt no doubt that Nicholas was more than a match for Jasper, as he certainly was bigger, and weighed twenty pounds more.

"My poor boy!" she said, pitifully, bending over her son; "are you much hurt?"

"Yes," said Nicholas; "and it's all on account of you!"

"I thought you were stronger than he."

"So I am, but he knows how to wrestle; besides, he's so quick."

"I thought you could have put him out easily."

"Well, don't set me to doing it again," said Thorne, sulkily. "I didn't want to fight. You made me."

"Don't mind it, my dear boy. It was because I was angry with him."

"Oh, how my head aches!"

"I'll put on some cologne. I'll give you an extra five dollars, too, for standing by your mother."

"All right, mother," said Thorne, in a more cheerful tone. "That's the way to talk. Give it to me now."

Jasper did not see either of them again that evening. He called on a friend, and, entering the house at ten o'clock, went directly to his own room.

CHAPTER XII.

A SCHEME OF VENGEANCE.

Mrs. Kent had never cared for Jasper. Since the marriage she had disliked him. Now that he had struck down Nicholas in her presence, she positively hated him. She did not stop to consider that he was provoked to it, and only acted in self-defense. She thirsted for revenge—more, indeed, than Nicholas, who, bully as he was, having been fairly worsted, was disposed to accept his defeat philosophically. If he could annoy or thwart Jasper he would have been glad to do it, but he did not desire to injure him physically.

Not so Mrs. Kent.

Her darling had been assaulted and defeated in her presence. She did not again wish to put him against Jasper lest he should be again defeated, but she wished Jasper, her detested step-son, to drink the same cup of humiliation which had been forced upon Nicholas.

So she sat pondering how to accomplish the object she had in view. She could not herself beat Jasper, though, had he been younger and smaller, she would certainly have attempted it. She must do it by deputy.

Under the circumstances she thought of Tom Forbes, a strong and stalwart hired man, who had been for some months working on the place. Probably he would not like the task, but she would threaten to discharge him if he refused to obey her commands, and this, she thought, would bring him around.

"I wonder where Jasper is?" said Nicholas, about eight o'clock, as he sat opposite the little table where his mother was sewing.

"Gone out, I suppose," said Mrs. Kent.

"He found the house too hot to hold him," suggested Thorne.

"He certainly will if he conducts himself in the future as he has already done. He makes a mistake if he thinks I will tolerate such conduct."

"It's because you're a woman," said her son. "Boys of his age don't make much account of women."

"Do you speak for yourself as well as for him?" asked Mrs. Kent, sharply.

"Of course not," said Nicholas, whose interest it was to keep on good terms with his mother. "Of course not; besides, you are my mother."

"You are much more of a gentleman than Jasper is," said his mother, appeased.

"I hope so," said Nicholas.

"As for him, I consider him a young ruffian."

"So he is," said Thorne, who was ready to assent to anything that his mother might say.

"And yet his father thought him a paragon!" continued Mrs. Kent, her lip curling. "It is strange how parents can be deceived!"

Unconsciously she illustrated the truth of this remark in her own person. She considered Nicholas handsome, spirited, and amiable—indeed, as an unusually fascinating and attractive boy. To others he was big, overgrown, malicious, and stupid. But then mothers are apt to look through different spectacles from the rest of the world.

"I guess Jasper'll want to change his guardian," said Thorne, laughing. "You and he won't hitch horses very well."

"Don't use such a common expression, Nicholas. I want you to grow up a well-bred gentleman."

"Oh, well, I mean to. But I say, if his father liked him so much, what made him appoint you to take care of him?"

"He didn't know how I felt toward Jasper. I humored his fancies, and treated him better than I felt toward him."

"Then you wanted to be his guardian?"

"Yes, I wanted to pay off old scores," said Mrs. Kent, again compressing her lips with unpleasant firmness.

"What made you dislike him?" asked her son, with curiosity.

"He was opposed to my marriage. He would have stopped it if he could, but there I got the better of him. When he found that he was too late he treated me with coldness. He never liked me."

"By Jove! I don't think he's had much reason," said Nicholas, laughing boisterously.

"He'll regret not having treated me with more attention. I can thwart all his plans and make his life very uncomfortable."

"I'll trust you to do that, mother. You've got spunk enough."

"Don't say 'spunk,' Nicholas."

"What shall I say, then?"

"Resolution—firmness."

"It's all the same."

"There is a choice in words. Remember, my dear boy, I want you to be a refined and cultivated gentleman."

"Well, I can be, now you're rich. But I say, mother, what are you going to do? You ain't going to stick down in this dull place all your life, are you?"

"No, Nicholas. In the summer we'll go travelling."

"Good!" exclaimed Nicholas, with satisfaction. "Where will we go?"

"How would you like to go to Niagara Falls?"

"Bully!"

"Or to Saratoga?"

"I don't know much about that."

"It is a fashionable place."

"Can a fellow have fun there?"

"Of course he can."

"Then I'd like to go. But I say, are you going to take Jasper, too?"

"No," said Mrs. Kent, decidedly. "I certainly shall not give him so much pleasure."

"I don't know. I might like it better if I had a fellow of my own age to go around with."

"You will find plenty of companions more agreeable than Jasper."

"All right, mother. I suppose you know best."

"You can trust me to provide for your happiness, Nicholas. It is all I live for."

The next morning Mrs. Kent arose early, and summoned the hired man, Tom Forbes.

"Tom," said she, "have you a good whip?"

"Yes, ma'am."

"And a strong arm?"

"Middlin', ma'am," answered the wondering hired man.

"I want you to be in the kitchen, provided with your whip, when breakfast is over."

"What for?" asked Tom, in surprise.

"Never mind now. I shall inform you at the time."

"All right, ma'am."

Twenty minutes later, Jasper, unaware of his step-mother's benevolent intentions, took his seat at the breakfast-table.

CHAPTER XIII.

MRS. KENT IS FOILED.

Breakfast was a quiet meal. Mrs. Kent preserved a frigid silence toward Jasper, interrupted only by necessary questions. Nicholas, who understood that there was a row in prospect, occasionally smiled as he looked across the table at Jasper, but he, too, was silent.

When breakfast was over, and the three arose from the table, Mrs. Kent said, in a cold voice:

"Jasper Kent, I have something to say to you."

"Very well," said Jasper, taking a seat and looking expectant.

"Yesterday you conducted yourself in a most improper manner."

"Please explain," said Jasper, quietly.

"You ought not to require any explanation. You made an assault upon Nicholas."

"I beg pardon, Mrs. Kent, but he made an assault upon me."

"You knocked him down."

"Not until he attacked me."

"He did so by my direction."

"Did you expect me to make no resistance?" asked Jasper.

"You had insulted me, and it was his duty, as my son, to resent it."

"I don't think you have any right to say that I insulted you, and you would not have any reason to complain of me if you would treat me with ordinary justice and politeness."

"You are insulting me now," said Mrs. Kent, angrily.

"I am telling the truth. I am sorry that it is the truth. I would prefer to live on good terms with you."

"And have your own way!" said his step-mother, sarcastically. "I understand you, but I will have you know that I am mistress in this house. Are you ready to apologize for having attacked Nicholas?"

"I did not wish to do it, especially as he didn't attack me of his own accord, but if he should do so again I should act in the same manner."

"Insolent!" exclaimed his step-mother, reddening.

"You have peculiar ideas of insolence," said Jasper, quietly. "I believe in defending myself, but I shouldn't like to harm Nicholas."

"You have undertaken to rebel against my authority," said Mrs. Kent, "but you don't understand me. I am not to be bullied or overcome by a boy."

"You are in no danger of either from me, madam."

"I shall take care not to give you the power. Nicholas, call Tom."

Jasper looked at his step-mother in amazement. What had Tom Forbes to do with their colloquy.

Nicholas opened the door of the adjoining room, the kitchen, and summoned the hired man.

Ignorant of why he was wanted, for Mrs. Kent had not informed him, he came into the room, and looked about with a perplexed expression.

He was a tall, strong-looking fellow, country-bred, of about twenty-five or six.

"Where is your whip, Tom?" demanded Mrs. Kent.

"My whip?" repeated Tom.

"Yes; didn't I tell you I wanted you to have it?"

"Yes, ma'am; it's in the kitchen."

"Bring it."

Tom went into the kitchen, and returned bringing the whip.

"What am I to do with it?" he asked.

"I will tell you in a moment. Jasper Kent," said his step-mother, turning to him, "you have rebelled against my just authority, you have insulted me in my own house, you have made a brutal attack upon my son in my presence, and now I am going to have you punished. Tom, I order you to give Jasper half a dozen lashes with your whip."

It is hard to tell which looked the more surprised at this brutal command, Jasper or the hired man. They looked at each other in amazement, but Tom did not stir.

"Did you hear me?" asked Mrs. Kent, sharply, impatient of the delay.

"Yes, ma'am, I heard you," answered Tom, slowly.

"Why don't you obey, then?" she continued, in the same tone.

"Because," said Tom, with manly independence, "I didn't hire out to do anything of the kind."

"Do you refuse?"

"Yes, I do. You may do your own dirty work."

"It seems you are not only disobedient, but insolent," said Mrs. Kent, angrily.

"You must be crazy, ma'am!" said the hired man, bluntly.

"No more of this. I discharge you from my employment."

"What! for not flogging Master Jasper?"

"For not obeying me."

"I'll follow your directions, ma'am, so far as they are in the line of duty, but I won't do that."

"I discharge you."

"As to that, ma'am, if I go, I'll let everybody in the village know why you sent me away."

For this Mrs. Kent was not altogether prepared. She knew that it was not prudent to defy public opinion. Perhaps she had already gone too far. She put a great constraint upon herself, and said:

"Go back to your work. I will speak of this matter hereafter."

Tom withdrew at once, glad of the opportunity. Thus far Mrs. Kent had been foiled, and she knew it. She could scarcely conceal her mortification.

Jasper, who had been passive thus far, now spoke. He felt outraged and disgusted by his step-mother's brutal purpose, though it had failed.

"Mrs. Kent," he said with quiet resolution, "after the scene of this morning I cannot remain in the same house with you. My father has not been dead a week, yet you have treated me in a manner which, though I never liked you, I could not have thought possible. You are left my guardian. I do not wish to remain another day in this house. Have I your permission to return to school?"

"No," said his step-mother.

"Why not?"

"Because you wish it. I do not mean to let you have your own way."

"I am willing to go to another school, if you insist upon it."

"You will go to no school. You will stay here."

"In this house?"

"Yes."

"With the opinion which you have of me, Mrs. Kent, I should hardly think this would be very agreeable to you."

"It will not. I hate the sight of you!" said his step-mother, with energy.

"I am sorry for that, but I am not surprised. From the way you have treated me, I should think so. Won't it be better for as both to be separated?"

"It will gratify your wishes, and therefore I order you to remain here."

"That we may have more such scenes as yesterday and to-day?"

"No; I am determined to break your rebellious will, and teach you to obey me implicitly."

"I have only to ask if you have fully made up your mind," said Jasper, quietly, but with suppressed excitement.

"I mean precisely what I say."

"Then, madam, I shall have to leave this house and go out into the world. I shall find more kindness among strangers than here."

"I have heard boys talk like this before," said Mrs. Kent, with contemptuous incredulity.

"Boys sometimes mean what they say," retorted Jasper.

He took his hat and left the room without another word.

"I say, mother," said Nicholas, "suppose he don't come back?"

"There's no fear of that," said Mrs. Kent, coldly.

"But I say, mother, he's pretty plucky, Jasper is."

"He won't run away from me as long as I have charge of his property, you may be sure of that. He'll be coming back and apologizing pretty soon."

"Suppose he doesn't?"

"Then it'll be his own fault."

"You may as well let him go back to school, mother. He'll be out of our way, and we can enjoy ourselves."

"I am not going to gratify him so far. He has defied me and insulted me, and he must take the consequences," said Mrs. Kent, with a compression of her thin lips.

On the whole, Jasper's prospects could not be said to be very flattering.

<h1 style="text-align:center">CHAPTER XIV.</h1>

<h2 style="text-align:center">MEDIATION.</h2>

When Jasper left the house he bent his steps to the dwelling of a friend of his father, Otis Miller, a man of considerable property and good position. He found Mr. Miller at home.

"I am glad to see you, Jasper," said he, cordially.

"Thank you, sir."

"You have met with a great loss," said Mr. Miller, attributing Jasper's serious expression to his father's death.

"Yes, sir; I am only just beginning to understand how much."

"A father's place cannot be supplied."

"No, sir; but this is not the extent of my trouble."

"Can I do anything to help you?"

"Yes, sir. I am very much in need of advice."

"I shall be glad to give you the best I can, Jasper. I was your father's friend, and I shall be glad to be yours also."

"Thank you, sir. My troubles are connected with my step-mother, who treats me like an enemy."

"Can this be so?" asked Mr. Miller, in surprise.

"I will tell you all, and then ask your advice."

"Do so."

Jasper told the story briefly and without excitement. It was only in his step-mother's presence that he felt disturbed.

"I have met your step-mother, but I know very little of her," said Mr. Miller. "She never impressed me very favorably, but I never dreamed that she would act in such an unreasonable manner. Perhaps even now matters are not as bad as you think. Sometimes people say things in anger which they repent of in their cooler moments."

"I don't think it is the case with Mrs. Kent."

"It is unfortunate, since she is your guardian."

"I wish you were my guardian, Mr. Miller."

"For your sake, Jasper, I wish I were. I don't think we should quarrel."

"I know we should not."

"You wish to know what to do?"

"Yes."

"You are quite sure you cannot stay at home?"

"I should be subject to constant persecution from Mrs. Kent."

"You think she would not allow you to go back to school?"

"She has refused to do so."

"There is one thing she cannot do, and that is, keep your portion of the estate from you when you become of age."

"No, I suppose not."

"You will then be rich."

"But the money won't do me any good now, will it?"

"In this way it will. Suppose I agree to pay your expenses at school—that is to say, advancing the money, to be repaid when you obtain yours?"

"That would be very kind, Mr. Miller; but I shouldn't like to subject you to that risk."

"You mean that a minor's promise would be invalid? Well, Jasper, I have too much confidence in you to have any doubt of your integrity."

"Thank you, Mr. Miller; but suppose I should die before attaining my majority?"

"Then I should probably lose the money."

"That is what I thought of. I should not like to have you run the risk."

"But I am willing to do so. However, it may be as well to ascertain definitely your step-mother's intentions first. I will call upon her in your interest and find out."

"Thank you, sir. I should like to have you do so, as I don't want to act too hastily."

"I will go at once. Will you remain here till I return?"

"Yes, sir."

When Mrs. Kent was told that Mr. Miller had called to see her she went down to meet him, not surmising his errand.

"Mrs. Kent," said he, after the ordinary greetings were over, "I have called with reference to your relations to your late husband's son, Jasper."

"Did he ask you to come?" demanded Mrs. Kent, frowning.

"No; but he came to ask my advice as to what he ought to do. I am sorry to hear that you are unfriendly."

"He has treated me with intolerable insolence," said Mrs. Kent, hotly.

"That surprises me. It is wholly contrary to his reputation with those who have known him from his infancy," said Mr. Miller, quietly.

"Then you don't know him as he is."

"He tells me you have accorded your own son superior privileges."

"My son treats me with respect."

"Probably you treat him differently from Jasper."

"I have reasons to."

"You will admit that it is aggravating to see a stranger—an intruder, I may say —preferred to him in his own home?"

"Who calls my son an intruder?" asked Mrs. Kent, hastily.

"Let us call him a stranger, then. Was Mr. Kent aware that you had a son?"

"I decline to answer your question," answered Mrs. Kent, with asperity.

"To pass on, then. Have you refused Jasper permission to return to the school at which his father placed him?"

"I have."

"May I ask why?"

"I don't know that I am responsible to you."

"Mrs. Kent," said Mr. Miller, gravely, "I was the friend of your late husband. I am the friend of his son, Jasper. As the friend of both, I ask you your reason."

"I will answer you, though I do not acknowledge your right to ask. I refuse to let Jasper go back to school, because I wish to punish him for his insolence and disobedience."

"It cannot be any satisfaction to you to have him at home, I should think."

"It is not. I have no reason to like his society."

"Then it appears that you punish yourself in keeping him here."

"Yes."

"Do you think, Mrs. Kent, that you have any right to deprive him of the opportunity to obtain an education?"

"He can attend school in this village," said Mrs. Kent.

"You know as well as I that there is neither a classical nor a high school here. He would be compelled to give up the course of study upon which he has commenced."

"That is his own fault," returned Mrs. Kent, doggedly.

"This, then, is your unalterable determination?"

"For the present, yes. If Jasper repents his ill-conduct, and makes up his mind to yield me that implicit obedience which is my due, I may hereafter consent to return him to school. But he must turn over a new leaf."

"Madam," said Mr. Miller, disgusted at the woman's manner, "do you consider that you are carrying out his father's wishes in reference to his son?"

"That is a question for me to decide," said Mrs. Kent, coldly. "I have undertaken the responsibility, and I have no fears about carrying out his wishes. I must trust my own judgment, not that of others."

"Madam," said Mr. Miller, after a pause, "there is one other question which I should like to put to you."

"Very well, sir."

"This guardianship imposed upon you is a certain amount of care. Are you willing to relinquish it to another?"

"To you, perhaps?" suggested Mrs. Kent, with a sneer.

"I should be willing to undertake it for Jasper's sake."

"I have no doubt you would, and I presume Jasper would be very glad to have you do so."

"I think he would, though he didn't authorize me to speak to you about it," said Mr. Miller.

"Then, sir, I refuse in the most emphatic terms. I shall not relinquish the power which his father's will gives me over him. He shall yet repent his insolence."

"I regret your animosity, Mrs. Kent," said Mr. Miller, with dignity, rising as he spoke. "I was inclined to think that Jasper had exaggerated his account of the difficulties. I see now that he was correct. I have only, in wishing you good-morning, to predict that you will yet regret the manner in which you have treated your step-son."

"I will take my chance of that," said Mrs. Kent. "You may report to Jasper that my only terms are unconditional submission."

"I will do so, madam; but you know, as well as I, what his answer will be. His nature is too manly to submit to tyranny, even from his step-mother."

"You are not over-polite, sir," said Mrs. Kent, angrily.

"I am truthful, madam," was the grave reply.

CHAPTER XV.
GOOD-BYE.

"Without exception, Jasper," said Mr. Miller, on his return, "I consider your step-mother the most disagreeble woman I ever met."

Jasper could not help smiling at the look of disgust upon the features of his father's friend.

"Then, sir, I infer that you did not succeed in your mission," he said.

"Succeed? No. She will offer no terms except unconditional submission on your part."

"That I won't agree to." said Jasper, promptly.

"I don't blame you—not a particle," said Mr. Miller.

"So much is settled, then," said Jasper. "Now the question comes up—what am I to do?"

"How old are you?"

"Nearly sixteen."

"Then five years must elapse before you come into possession of your property?"

"Yes, sir."

"And for that length of time you are to be under the guardianship of Mrs. Kent?"

"Yes, sir."

"It is unfortunate," said the old gentleman, shrugging his shoulders. "I took the liberty to suggest to your step-mother that if the cares of a guardian should prove burdensome to her I would assume them."

"What did she say?"

"She replied in a sarcastic manner, and avowed her determination to remain your guardian."

"What would you advise me to do, then, Mr. Miller?"

"Before answering, Jasper, I will tell you a secret."

Jasper looked curious.

"Your father left in my hands a paper to be opened two years after his death. It undoubtedly relates to you."

"What do you think it is?"

"It may relate to the guardianship, but that is only conjecture."

"Does my step-mother know of this?"

"Neither she nor anyone else, save you and myself."

"It will do us no good at present?"

"No; but it influences my advice. Go to school for the next two years. I will advance the money to pay your bills. If at the end of that time the paper is what I hope it is, you will then be able to pay me, and for the balance of your minority I can become your guardian."

"I wish you might, Mr. Miller; but I don't think, under the circumstances, I want to go back to school."

"What do you wish to do, Jasper?"

"I am young, and I would like to see something of the world. I would like to imagine myself a poor boy, as I really am just now, and see if I cannot make my own way."

"I hardly know what to say to that, Jasper. I am afraid you do not appreciate the difficulties in your way."

"To battle against them will make me strong."

"Suppose you get in a tight place?"

"Then I will write to you for help."

"That's better. On this condition I will make no further opposition to your wishes. But have you any money?"

"Ten dollars."

"Rather a small sum to begin the world with."

"Yes, sir. If you are willing to lend me fifty more I think I can get along till I can earn some."

"Willingly. Where do you propose to go?"

"To the West. My father has a cousin, a lady, married, and living in a small town on the banks of the Mississippi. I have never been to the West. I should like to go out there and see if I can't find some employment in that neighborhood."

"I suppose I must not object, but your plan appears to me rather quixotic."

"You might not have thought so at my age, Mr. Miller."

"No; we look upon such things differently as we grow older. When do you want to start?"

"To-morrow."

"Stay at my house till then."

"Thank you, sir. I will go home this afternoon and get my carpet-bag and a few underclothes, and then I shall be ready to start to-morrow morning."

Jasper did as proposed. He would gladly have dispensed with this call at the house which had once been a home to him, but was so no longer; but it was necessary to make it.

He caught sight of Tom Forbes near the house.

"Tom," he called out, "do you know if Mrs. Kent is at home?"

"No, Master Jasper, she went out riding, and her cub went with her."

"I am afraid you're not respectful, Tom," said Jasper, laughing.

"He don't deserve respect. He puts on as many airs as a prince. I warrant he was poor enough before his mother took him home. What do you think he said to me?"

"What was it?"

"'Look here, Tom, you harness the horse right up, do you hear? Don't stand dawdling there, for I and mother are going out to ride.'"

"That sounds like Nicholas."

"You may be sure he ain't used to prosperity, or he wouldn't put on so many airs!"

"Well, Tom, I'm glad Mrs. Kent is out. I don't want to meet her, nor Nicholas, either."

"You'll see 'em at supper, won't you?"

"No; I shall not be here to supper."

"When are you coming back?"

"Not at all."

"You don't mean that, Master Jasper?"

"Yes, I do."

"Are you going to school?"

"No; I'm going out West."

"Out West?" exclaimed Tom Forbes, stopping work in surprise.

"Yes, Tom, I'm going out there to seek my fortune."

"But there ain't any need of that, Master Jasper. Didn't your father leave you a fortune?"

"I'm not to have it till I'm twenty-one, and till then my step-mother is my guardian. Now, I put it to you, Tom, can I stay at home to be treated as you saw me treated this morning?"

"No, you can't, that's a fact. Master Jasper, I wish you'd take me with you as your servant."

"As to that, Tom, I am in no position to have a servant; I've got to work for my own living."

"And she here living on the fat of the land!" exclaimed Tom, indignantly. "It's an outrageous shame!"

"Strong language, Tom," said Jasper, smiling. "Mind my amiable step-mother doesn't hear you."

"I don't care if she does."

"Thank you for your offer, Tom, but I must go alone. Perhaps I shall prosper out there. I hope so, at any rate."

"Have you got any money, Master Jasper? I've got a few dollars laid by. If they'll do you any good you're welcome to take 'em. I shan't need 'em."

"Thank you, Tom," said Jasper, cordially grasping his toil-embrowned hand, "but I am well provided for. Mr. Miller, my father's friend, is mine, too. He has lent me some money, and will lend me more if I need it."

"I'm glad of that. You'll always find friends."

Half an hour later, as Jasper was going up the street, with his carpet-bag in one hand, he saw the open carriage approaching in which Mrs. Kent and Nicholas were seated. He would liked to have escaped observation, but there was no chance.

"Why, there's Jasper!" said Nicholas, "and he's got a carpet-bag in his hand."

"Stop the carriage!" said Mrs. Kent, peremptorily.

Nicholas, who was driving, obeyed.

"Have you been to the house?" asked the step-mother.

"Yes," said Jasper.

"What does that carpet-bag mean?"

"It means that I am going away."

"Where? As your guardian, I demand to know!"

"As my guardian, will you provide for my expenses?"

"No."

"Then I don't feel called upon to tell you."

"You will repent this insubordination," said Mrs. Kent, angrily. "You will yet return home in rags."

"Never!" answered Jasper, with emphasis. "Good-afternoon, Mrs. Kent."

"Drive on, Nicholas!" said Mrs. Kent, angrily. "How I hate that boy!" she ejaculated.

"It strikes me, mother, you've got the best of it," said Nicholas. "You've got his property, and as to his company, we can do without that."

CHAPTER XVI.

AN UNPLEASANT ADVENTURE.

A week later Jasper was one of the passengers on a train bound for St. Louis, and already within sixty miles of that flourishing city. He had stopped over at Niagara and Cincinnati—a day or so at each place. He gratified his desire to see the great cataract, and felt repaid for doing so, though the two stops trenched formidably upon his small capital. Indeed, at the moment when he is introduced anew to the reader's notice he had but ten dollars remaining of the sum with which he started. He was, however, provided, besides, with a through ticket to St. Louis.

He had been sitting alone, when a stranger entering the car seated himself in the vacant seat.

Looking up, Jasper noticed that he was a tall man, shabbily dressed, with thin, sallow face and a swelling in the left cheek, probably produced by a quid of tobacco.

"Good-mornin', colonel," said the stranger, sociably.

"Good-morning, sir," said Jasper, smiling. "I haven't the honor of being a colonel."

"Haven't you, cap'n? Well, that ain't of no account. It'll come in time. Where are you travelling?"

"To St. Louis."

"Ever been there afore?"

"No; this will be my first visit."

"You don't say! Where may you be from?"

"From New York State," answered Jasper, amused.

The stranger drew from his pocket a package of chewing tobacco and passed it politely to Jasper.

"Help yourself, colonel," he said hospitably.

"No, thank you; I don't chew."

"Shoo, you don't say so! High time you began, then."

"I don't think I shall ever form the habit of chewing."

"Yes, you will, colonel; everybody does. Travellin' on business?"

"Well, not exactly," said Jasper, hesitatingly. "That is, I am looking for a chance to go into business."

"Got any capital?" interjected the stranger, carelessly, squirting a yellow stream upon the floor of the car.

"Oh, I don't expect to go into business for myself at present," said Jasper, amused at the thought.

"No?" said the other, reflectively. "If you had five thousand dollars I might take you into partnership."

"What is your business?" asked Jasper, with curiosity.

"Cotton," said the stranger. "I'm a cotton broker. I do a large business."

"You don't look like it," thought Jasper, looking at his shabby costume.

"You don't want a clerk, do you?" asked our hero.

"Well, no, colonel. There ain't any vacancy now in my establishment. May be soon."

Had Jasper felt favorably impressed with his companion he would have inquired where in the city his place of business might be, but it did not strike him that he should care to be in his employ.

He accordingly pulled out a copy of a popular magazine which he had bought the day before, and began to read. The stranger bought a paper of the train-boy, and engaged in a similar way. Fifteen minutes passed in this way. At the end of that time the stranger rose leisurely, and with a brief "Mornin', colonel," passed out of the car. Whether he got into the next one or got out at the station which they were approaching Jasper could not distinguish, nor did he feel specially interested in the matter.

The time soon came when he felt his interest increased.

A few miles further on the conductor entered the car.

It was one of his usual rounds to look at tickets.

When he came up to Jasper, he said:

"Be lively now. Let me see your ticket."

"Isn't it in my hat?" asked Jasper, taking it off.

"No; did you put it there?"

"I thought I did," said our hero, surprised. "It was there when you last passed round."

"Look in your pockets."

Jasper felt in all of them, but the missing ticket could not be found.

"It may have fallen on the floor," he said, and rising he looked under the seat.

But in vain.

"Did you have any ticket?" asked the conductor, suspiciously.

"Certainly. You have looked at it yourself several times."

"You are mistaken; I got on at the last station."

"I have come all the way from Cincinnati," said Jasper, uncomfortably. "I couldn't have come so far without a ticket. What shall I do?"

"You'll have to pay from the last station to St. Louis."

This was not very agreeable in the state of Jasper's finances.

"How much is it?" he asked.

"Two dollars."

Jasper felt for his pocket-book, when a new surprise awaited him. A look of consternation swept over his countenance.

His pocket-book was gone.

"Don't keep me waiting," said the conductor, impatiently.

"My pocket-book is gone!" exclaimed our hero, gazing in blank dismay at the expectant official.

"What?"

"I can't find my pocket-book."

"Look here, young man," said the conductor, roughly, "that's too thin."

"It's true!" said Jasper.

"It won't go down, young man. I've seen such customers as you before. You're a beat!"

"A what?"

"A beat—a dead-beat, if you prefer it. Off you go at the next station!"

Jasper was greatly alarmed at the unexpected turn affairs had taken.

"Let me go to St. Louis, and I'll get money to pay you."

"It's no use," said the conductor, inexorably. "My orders are strict. If you can't pay, you can't ride."

"But my pocket was picked," said Jasper, new light flashing upon him. "There was a stranger who sat beside me a while ago. He must have taken my ticket and money, too."

"Of course there was," said the conductor, with sarcasm. "That's the way it usually happens. I'm used to such games, young man. It won't do you any good. Out you go!"

"Let me go through the cars and see if I can't find the man that robbed me. I'd know him in a minute."

"Well," said the conductor, relenting slightly, "be quick about it."

Jasper waited for no more. He rose from his seat and, carpet-bag in hand, passed into the next car.

It proved to be the smoking car.

Groups of men were playing cards, and, as Jasper judged, were playing for money. Among them, to his great joy, he recognized his shabby companion, the cotton broker of St. Louis. The latter was playing with three other men, black-bearded, and loud both in their dress and speech.

Without a moment's hesitation Jasper advanced and touched his late companion on the shoulder.

The latter looked up, and without a sign of recognition said:

"What's wanted, sir?"

For the first time it struck Jasper that his errand was rather an awkward one. How could he ask this man if he had taken his property?

"I beg your pardon, sir," said he, "but did you see anything of my ticket and money?"

"What do you mean, stranger?"

"You were sitting by me a little while ago, in the rear car."

"I don't remember it."

"And I thought you might have seen my pocket-book and ticket."

"Well, I didn't," said the other, fiercely. "What made you think I did?"

"I can't find them."

"I don't know anything about them. General, it's your deal."

He turned abruptly away from Jasper, and the boy slowly withdrew to a little distance, sorely puzzled. On the one hand, he felt convinced that this man had abstracted his ticket and money. On the other, he doubted whether it would be safe to charge him with it.

While he was hesitating, the cars began to go more slowly.

The conductor entered the car.

"Have you found your ticket?" he asked.

"No."

"Then leave the train at this next stopping-place."

Jasper had no chance to remonstrate. Obeying necessity, he stepped upon the platform, and the train swept on.

CHAPTER XVII.

THE DESERTED HOUSE.

To be without money is far from pleasant under any circumstances, but to be penniless a thousand miles from home, in the midst of strangers, is far worse. Jasper found himself in this position so unexpectedly that as he stood beside the little depot with his carpet-bag in his hand he felt utterly bewildered.

He looked around him.

Not a house was in sight. Why the railroad company should have established a depot there he could not understand. Probably there must be some village not far away.

No other passenger had got out with Jasper. There was no other person in sight but the station-master, a tall, sallow-faced man, in a slouched hat, who eyed our hero curiously.

Jasper approached him.

"What place is this?" he asked.

"Don't you know?" questioned the man.

"No."

"What made you stop here, then?"

Jasper hesitated. There seemed no use in taking this man into his confidence.

"I am going to take a look at the village. I suppose there is a village?"

"Well," drawled the man, "there's some houses back."

"What's the name of the place?"

"Croyden."

"How far back is the village?"

"A matter of two miles."

"Is it easy to find the way?"

"There's the road."

The station-master pointed out a road leading through woods.

"Thank you," said Jasper.

"You don't happen to have any 'baccy with you?" asked the station-master.

"No, I am sorry to say."

"I thought maybe you might. I'm most out."

Jasper took the road indicated by his informant and pressed on.

When he had walked half a mile along the lonely road he stopped suddenly and asked himself:

"What are my plans? What use is there in going to Croyden?"

It was a hard question to answer.

Still, he must go somewhere. He could not go to St. Louis without money, and there was a bare possibility that he might find something to do in Croyden. If he could earn a few dollars he could go on, and once in a large city there would be hope of permanent employment.

How different would have been his situation if he had not lost his money, and how unfortunate it was that he should have been set down at this dismal place!

He kept on, meeting no one.

Finally he came to a place where the road divided into two forks or branches, one leading to the right, the other to the left.

"Which shall I take?" he asked himself.

There seemed no choice so far as he could see. Neither was very promising, nor was there any sign-post to inform him of what he wished to know.

"I wish somebody would come along," thought Jasper.

But nobody did.

Forced to decide, he decided in favor of the left-hand road, and walked on.

After a while he began to suspect that he had made a wrong decision. The road became little more than a lane, and seemed unfrequented. But just as he was going to turn back he espied at some distance from the road a rude dwelling, which, from its weather-beaten appearance, seemed never to have been painted.

"I can find out something there, at any rate," thought Jasper, and he bent his steps toward it.

Brief time brought him in front of the house. It was certainly a quiet-looking place.

"It must be dismal to live here," thought Jasper.

He knocked with his fist at the door. On account of the smallness of the house the knock certainly must have been heard, but there was no response.

"The people must be deaf," thought Jasper.

He knocked again, this time considerably louder, and waited for some one to answer his summons.

He waited in vain.

"It must be a deserted house," thought our hero. "I have a great mind to explore it—that is, if I can get in."

He tried the door, and, a little to his surprise, it yielded to his touch. The door being in the centre of the house, there was a room on each side. The door to the left; opened into a room which was quite bare of furniture. On the other side, however, was a room containing a table and three chairs. On the table was a dirty clay-pipe and a box of tobacco, and there was a dead odor of tobacco-smoke lingering in the closely-shut room.

"That looks as if there were somebody living here," thought Jasper.

"Halloo!" he shouted, raising his voice.

He felt that it would be better to make his presence known, as otherwise he might be suspected of entering the house with burglarious designs, though it would have puzzled a burglar to find anything worth purloining.

"There can't be anybody in the house or I should have been heard," thought our hero. "However, I'll call again."

This time there was a faint sound that came to his ears. It seemed like the voice of a child.

"Where did that come from?" Jasper considered.

And he waited to hear if it would be repeated.

It was repeated, and now he could make out that it came from above.

"I'll go up," he decided.

He climbed the rude staircase, and pushed open the door of the room above the one in which he had been standing a moment before. He gazed in wonder at the spectacle before him.

A boy, five years of age, who in spite of his frightened expression possessed great personal beauty, was lying on a bed in one corner of the room. He looked at Jasper in uncertainty at first, then with confidence, and said:

"Did you come for me?"

"Do you live here?" asked Jasper, in surprise, for this boy was not at all like the children usually to be found in such houses as this.

His complexion was of dazzling whiteness, his hair was a bright chestnut, and his clothing was such as wealthy parents can afford to give to their children.

"Do you live here?" repeated Jasper.

"No," said the child.

"How came you here, then?"

"Big man—big, ugly man brought me."

"When?"

"I don't know," said the child.

He was evidently too young to measure the lapse of time.

"Was it yesterday?"

"No; long ago."

"I suppose it seems long to him," thought Jasper.

"Is there nobody else in the house?" asked Jasper.

"There's a woman," said the little boy.

"Is she the wife of the man who took you away?"

But this question the little boy did not seem to comprehend.

"Have you got a mother?" asked Jasper.

"Take me to mamma," said the little fellow, stretching out his arms, and beginning to cry. "I want to see my mamma."

Jasper advanced to the bed.

He began to understand that the boy had been kidnapped, and he felt great compassion for him.

He tried to raise the boy from the bed and take him in his arms, when he made an unexpected discovery.

The boy's ankles were firmly tied by a rope, which connected with the bedpost, so that it was impossible for him to leave the bed.

"Who did this?" asked Jasper, indignantly. "Who tied you?"

"It was the man—the big, ugly man," answered the child.

"I will soon unfasten you," said Jasper, and he set to work untying the knot.

"Will you take me home?" asked the little boy.

"Yes," said Jasper, soothingly, "I'll take you home."

But just as he had completed his task he heard steps upon the stairs. What if it were the man of whom the child spoke!

Jasper threw one arm around the child, and with his teeth set hard fixed his eyes expectantly upon the door.

CHAPTER XVIII.
THE KIDNAPPED CHILD.

The woman who entered was of middle size, dressed in a cheap print, dirty and faded, which corresponded very well with her general aspect. She looked weary and worn, and moved languidly as if she had little interest in life. She looked startled at the sight of Jasper, and pressed her hand to her heart.

"Who are you?" she asked.

"A stranger," answered our hero.

"How came you here?"

"I suppose I ought to apologize for being here, but I knocked twice and got no answer. That made me think the house was deserted. I entered, and hearing a low cry, came to this room."

The woman sank into a chair near the door.

"Is this your child?" asked Jasper, in his turn.

The woman answered hesitatingly, after a pause:

"No."

"I knew he could not be. How did he come here?'

"My husband brought him here," answered the woman, with some hesitation.

"Is he any relation to you?"

"N-no."

"Is he boarding here?"

"Yes."

The woman's hesitation increased Jasper's suspicion. He said:

"I found the boy tied to the bedpost. Did you tie him?"

"Yes."

"Why did you do that?"

"I thought he might slip off while I was out I went out for some water. That is the reason I did not answer your knock."

"Madam," said Jasper, coming to the point, "you may answer me or not; but if you do, tell the truth. Was not this child stolen?"

The woman looked nervous and frightened, and moved restlessly in her chair.

"Don't blame me," she said. "It wasn't my fault."

"Whose was it, then?"

"It was my husband's."

"Then the child was stolen?"

"Yes."

"I suppose your husband kidnapped the child in order to get money from the parents for his return?"

"Yes," the woman admitted.

"How can you assist him in such wicked practices?"

"What can I do?" said the woman, helplessly. "I have spoken to him, but it does no good. He won't heed anything that I say."

Jasper began to pity the poor woman. It looked as if she were an unwilling helper in her husband's crimes.

"Do you know where your husband got this boy from?" he asked.

"No; he didn't tell me."

"Is this the first child he has kidnapped?"

"I ought not to speak against my husband," said the woman, uneasily, appearing to think that she had already told too much.

"Yes, you ought. Otherwise you will be as bad as he."

"He will beat me."

"Does he ever do that?" asked Jasper, compassionately.

"He is very rough sometimes," said the wife, shrinking.

"I am sorry for you," said Jasper, gently. "Where is your husband now?"

"He went out this morning. Perhaps he is hunting. He never tells me where he is going."

"When do you expect him back?"

"I can't tell. He may be here in five minutes; he may not be here before night."

"In that case," thought Jasper, "I had better be off as soon as possible. I should be no match for this brute in human form. Judging from what I have heard of him, he would kill me without scruple if he thought I were interfering with his plans."

"How long has this child been here?" he asked.

"Three or four days."

"I am going to take him away," proceeded Jasper, fixing his eyes earnestly upon the woman, to see how she took the proposal.

"No, no!" she exclaimed, quickly. "My husband won't allow it."

"He won't know it."

"It won't do," she continued, rapidly. "He would kill you if he overtook you."

This was a serious consideration, truly. Jasper had no weapons, and a boy of his age would have been a poor match for a strong man, as the kidnapper probably was.

"After all, I had better not interfere," he thought. "It can do no good, and will only expose me to great danger."

But just at this instant the little boy's soft hand slid into his, and he could not resist the touching appeal for his protection.

"I shall take the risk," he said. "I can't leave the boy here. I will try to find his parents and restore him to them."

He had scarcely said this when the woman, who had casually glanced out of the window, started up in alarm, exclaiming:

"There is my husband coming! Oh, what shall we do?"

CHAPTER XIX.
A BRUTE IN HUMAN SHAPE.

Jasper could not help feeling that he was in rather a critical position. A man whose business it was to kidnap young children in order to extort money from their friends was not likely to be very scrupulous, and the fear of having his secret divulged might lead him to extreme measures.

"Is your husband likely to come up here?" he asked.

"I don't know; he may," answered the woman, anxiously.

"Can't you hide me?" suggested Jasper.

"Yes, yes," she said, recovering something of her presence of mind. "There, get into that closet. I'll come and let you out when he is gone."

She opened the door of a closet in one corner of the room. It was quite dark inside, and except a stool, it was entirely empty.

"Sit down there," said the woman. "I must go down now."

She buttoned the door, and our hero found himself a close prisoner in the dark. It certainly gave him a peculiar sensation. Only a week before he had been at his Eastern home. Now he was more than a thousand miles away, penniless, and a prisoner. But though he was peculiarly situated, he was not discouraged. In fact, with a brave boy's love of adventure, he felt a certain exhilaration and wondered what was coming next. His courage and enterprise rose with the occasion, and he began to consider what course he should take after he got out.

While he is sitting in the closet in dark captivity, we will go below and make acquaintance with the man whose arrival had produced so great a sensation.

Before going down, the woman said to the child:

"Don't tell anybody about the boy in the closet."

"No, I won't," said the child, obediently.

The woman hurried down stairs, but her husband was already waiting for her.

He was a black-browed ruffian, with a rough beard of a week's growth. He threw himself sullenly into a chair and growled:

"Where were you? You're always out of the way when I come home."

"I just went up stairs a minute, Dick," she answered.

"To see the brat, I suppose."

"Yes."

"I've a great mind to knock him on the head."

"Oh, Dick, you wouldn't injure the little innocent," she said, earnestly.

"Wouldn't I? I would if I was paid enough, but there's nothing to be made by killing him."

"Thank heaven!" uttered the woman, fervently.

"You haven't got the heart of a chicken!" said the man, contemptuously. "Give me something to eat. I'm hungry."

The woman began to bustle around in obedience to his command.

"I haven't got much in the house, Dick," she said, apologetically.

"What have you got?" he growled.

"Some eggs and a little bacon. Shall I make you some tea?"

"No; bring out the whisky."

"There's none left, Dick."

The man uttered an oath expressive of disappointment.

"Well, give me some slops, then," he said. "I must have something to drink."

"Didn't you shoot anything?" she ventured to ask.

"I haven't been hunting."

"I thought you took out your gun."

"What if I did? I don't always hunt when I take my gun. I expected to hear from the friends of that brat this morning, but I didn't. They must hurry up with their money if they don't want me to strangle him."

"Perhaps they didn't get your letter, Dick."

"Yes, they did. I took care of that. I s'pose they're hatching up some plot to have me arrested. If they do, it'll be a bad day for the brat."

He looked fierce and brutal enough to execute the dark threat at which he indirectly hinted. There was a cruel look in his eye which showed that he would have had small scruples about injuring an innocent child, if provoked by the desire for revenge.

While his wife was cooking the eggs he filled his pipe and began to smoke. She made all the haste she could, knowing that her husband was far from patient. Soon the frugal repast was ready. She set it on the table, and said:

"It's all ready, Dick. Better eat it while it's hot."

"I'll eat it when I choose," he growled, in his usual spirit of contradiction.

However, he was hungry, and laying aside his pipe, did as she requested. Soon he had dispatched all the food set before him.

"There isn't enough to keep a kitten from starving," he said.

"I'm sorry, Dick."

"Much you are sorry," he growled. "A pretty wife you are."

"I wish there were more. If you'll give me some money I'll go out and buy something."

"Money!" he snarled. "You're always wanting money. Do you think I am made of money?"

"No, Dick; but you know I have none. I wish I knew of any way to earn it."

"You do?"

"Yes, Dick."

"Then I suppose you'd be leaving me," he said, suspiciously.

"No, I wouldn't. You know I wouldn't, Dick."

"So you say," he answered, brutally, "How's the brat? Has it been crying?"

"No; it is a very good child."

"I'll go up and take a look at it."

He arose from his seat, and advanced toward the door.

His wife followed him.

"Where are you going?" he asked, turning upon her.

"I'm going up, too," she answered, meekly.

"What for? Can't you trust me with the brat?"

"Yes, Dick, but it isn't much used to you. You might frighten it, and make it cry."

"That's all right," he answered, smiling grimly. "I like to hear children cry."

"How can you enjoy the sufferings of a child?"

"Halloo! What's that?" he said, looking sharply at her. "You dare to find fault with me, do you?"

"I didn't mean that, Dick," she said, submissively.

"It's lucky you didn't," he said, warningly. "I don't allow none of that, wife or no wife."

"May I go up?"

"If you want to."

So the two went up stairs together.

The wife was nervous lest the child in some way might excite the suspicions of her husband and betray the presence of Jasper. She felt, therefore, very ill at ease.

The child was sitting up in bed.

"Halloo, young 'un, how yer gettin' along?" asked the man, roughly.

The child did not answer, but looked frightened.

"Why don't you answer?" demanded the man, frowning.

The child looked toward the woman, and seemed on the point of crying.

"Can't you say something to the gentleman?" said the woman, soothingly.

Thus adjured, the little boy said:

"Won't you take me to my mamma?"

"Oh, yes, I'll take you as soon as your mamma sends me some money," said the man named Dick, "and she'd better do it pretty soon, too," he muttered.

He threw himself into a chair, and ceased to notice the child.

"Do you know, old woman," he said in a different tone, "I've heard news that'll rather take you by suprise?"

"I hope it is good news," said his wife, anxiously.

"Well, that's as may be," he answered. "It ought to be good news for us, but there's no saying. You know my sister?"

"Mrs. Thorne?"

"Yes. Well, she's had a stroke of luck."

"How was that?"

"Well, you see she went as governess into a family. The man was rich and an invalid—a widower, too. What does she do but get him to marry her?"

"She has been fortunate."

"That isn't all of it. She hadn't been married but two or three months when her husband died, leaving her a third of his property and guardian to his son, who inherits the rest. So she's a rich woman. I say she ought to do something for her brother Dick. Don't you say so?"

"I think she would be willing," said the wife.

"She ought to be, but she's selfish. She always was. If only I had the money I'd go East, and see what I could get out of her."

"You'd take me with you, Dick?"

"No, I wouldn't. It'll be all I can do to raise money enough to pay my own expenses, let alone yours. If I get anything I'll come back, and you'll get your share. That's why I want the parents of that brat to fork over the cash pretty quick."

"How did you learn the news about your sister, Dick?"

"An old pal of mine has just come from that way and told me all about it."

Every word of this dialogue was beard by Jasper in his place of concealment. He was astonished beyond measure to learn that this ruffian was the brother of his step-mother.

"No wonder I don't like her," he thought, "if they have any traits in common. What a fate, for my kind and gentle father to marry the sister of such a man!"

"I'm glad of it," said his wife.

"Well, so am I, if she'll do the right thing by me; but if she don't, then I'm sorry."

"What shall I do when you're away, Dick?"

"Get along as well as you can. Folks'll give you victuals, if you get hard up."

"I don't like to beg."

"Wish me good luck, then, and money enough to take care of you. What are you starin' at, young 'un?"

This he said to the child, whose eyes, as if by a species of fascination, were fixed upon him.

"Take me home to mamma!" pleaded the child, beginning to cry.

"Shut up!" said the ruffian, harshly, striding to the bed and pinching the boy's arm till he cried with the pain.

"Oh, don't, Dick," pleaded the woman, who was fond of children, though she had never been a mother.

"I'll give the brat something to cry for," said her husband, and he pinched him again.

"Oh, Dick, how can you torture the poor child?" said his wife, braver in the little boy's defence than in her own.

"What business has it to cry, then? I'd like to choke it. If you don't hush I'll serve you the same way."

Jasper had listened to this brutality as long as he could, but his indignation became too hot to be repressed. Thoughtless of consequences, he burst open the closet door and strode into the presence of the astonished ruffian, his fists involuntarily clenched, and his eyes kindling with indignation.

CHAPTER XX.
A STRANGE COMMISSION.

The man whom we have called Dick stopped short and gazed in astonishment at the boy who had so fearlessly stepped upon the scene.

"Where did you come from?" he demanded, frowning.

"From that closet," answered Jasper.

"How came you there? What business have you in my house, anyway?" demanded the ruffian.

"I entered it supposing it to be deserted," said Jasper. "While I was below I heard that poor boy cry, and came up."

"Did you know he was here?" asked the ruffian, turning to his wife, and speaking menacingly.

"Yes, Dick."

"Why did you let him in?"

"He came in while I was out."

"Why didn't you tell me he was here?"

"Because I didn't want him injured in any way. I was afraid you would be angry with him."

"That is where you are right," said Dick, adding an oath. "The young scoundrel shall pay for his impudence in entering my house like a thief."

"You have no right to say that," said Jasper. "I have explained to you why I came here."

"You hid in the closet, intending to come out and steal when we were out of the way."

"What could I steal?" asked Jasper, looking around him.

"Do you mean to taunt me with my poverty?" exclaimed the ruffian, enraged.

"No; I am poorer than you."

"You look like it."

"It is true. I was robbed in the cars by a pickpocket, and because I was penniless and could not pay my fare I was put off at this station."

"Is this true?" demanded Dick, with a searching look.

"Yes; I wish it were not."

"How came you near this house?"

"I set out to walk to the village, and must have lost my way."

"Why did you come out of that closet?" was the next demand.

"Because I heard you abusing that little boy," said Jasper, fearlessly.

"I have a right to do what I please to my own child."

"It isn't your child."

"What do you mean by that, you impudent young jackanapes?"

Unobserved by her husband, the wife made a warning sign to Jasper not to provoke the man, whose evil passion she so well knew.

Jasper comprehended the sign, but it did not influence him. Frank and fearless by temperament, he thought it his duty to stand between the little boy and this ruffian's brutality. Still he appreciated the woman's kindness, and resolved to bear it in mind. Indeed, he saw that she was rather to be pitied than blamed.

Her natural instincts were good, but she was under the control of a bad man.

"I heard what you were saying," said Jasper.

"You heard?"

"Yes, while I was in the closet."

"What did you hear, you young scoundrel?" demanded the ruffian.

"Enough to satisfy me that you have stolen this boy from his parents."

"It's a lie!"

"No; it is the truth. I felt sure of it before, and now I know it. You took him in order to extort money from his friends."

"Well," said the ruffian, defiantly, "what if I did? Have you anything to say against it?"

"Yes," said Jasper.

"I shall have to wring your neck by and by," muttered Dick. "Well, go on. Spit out what you've got to say."

"I say it's a cruel wrong to the parents," said Jasper, boldly, "and to the child also. But you make it worse when you try to abuse the boy."

"Come, boy, if you care so much for the brat, suppose you take his place, and take the beating I was going to give him," suggested the ruffian, mockingly.

"I would rather suffer than have him suffer," said Jasper, quietly; "but perhaps you will change your mind when you hear what I have to say."

"Oh, you are going to beg off!" sneered the ruffian, with a look of satisfaction. "I thought you'd come to your senses."

"You are mistaken as to my intention. I want to speak to you about your sister —formerly Mrs. Thorne."

"What do you know about her?" asked the man, in extreme astonishment.

"A good deal. She is my step-mother."

"What! Are you the son of the man she married?" asked Dick, eagerly.

"I am Jasper Kent."

"That's the name. So she sent you out to me, did she? That's better than I thought She hasn't forgotten her brother, after all."

"No; you are mistaken," said Jasper. "She never so much as told me she had a brother."

Dick looked disappointed. Then, with sudden suspicion, he said, roughly:

"I believe you are lying. This Jasper Kent is rich—the heir of two-thirds of his father's property. You say you are penniless."

"That is true. Both stories are true. I am my father's principal heir, but your sister is my guardian. She has treated me in such a way that I left the house."

"Ran away, eh?"

"No, I gave her full notice of what I should do. I told her that if I were decently treated I would stay, but if she continued to insult me, and give the preference in all things to her own boy, Nicholas, I would go away."

"You haven't been such a fool as to go off and leave all your property in her hands?"

"I shall come in possession of it when I am twenty-one. Till then I will try to support myself."

"Come, boy, you're plucky. I'm glad you came, after all. I want to hear more about my sister's affairs. Come down stairs, and we'll talk."

Dick appeared suddenly to have forgotten his animosity. He became even friendly in his manner, as he gave our hero this invitation.

"Old woman," said he, addressing his wife, "can't you rake up something for this boy to eat? I dare say he is hungry."

"I don't think we've got anything more in the house."

"I'll go out directly and get something. Come down, boy, I want to ask you a few more questions."

They went down stairs, followed by the wife. She was happily relieved by the unexpected good understanding between her husband and Jasper.

"Now tell me," said Dick, eagerly, when they were in the lower room, "how much property has my sister got?"

"Probably between thirty and forty thousand dollars."

"As much as that?" said Dick, complacently. "Well, she has feathered her nest well."

"I don't like Mrs. Kent," said Jasper. "Though she is your sister, I am obliged to say that, but it is not at all on account of the property my father left her. If he had given her one-half his estate I would not have complained, as long as she treated me fairly."

"Helen was always a hard customer. She's got a will of her own," chuckled Dick.

"There was no hope of our getting on together," said Jasper.

"She ought to do something for me—don't you think so? I'm her only brother."

"As to that," said Jasper, "my opinion wouldn't have any weight with her. If you are poor and need help, it would be only natural for her to help you."

"That's the way to talk! You won't say anything against me to her?"

"Certainly not," said Jasper. "I shall not write to her at all; and even if I did, I wouldn't try to interfere with her disposing of her property in any way she thinks best."

"Come, you're a trump, after all. I like you. You're plucky, too."

"Thank you."

"I'll say a good word for you to my sister when I see her."

"You'd better not," said Jasper. "If she thinks you are friendly to me you'll stand a poor chance of any favors. Better abuse me."

Dick roared with laughter.

"I say, youngster, you're a smart 'un. I see you're friendly by your hint. I'll abuse you to her, never fear. You must take a drink on that. Say, old woman, where's the whisky?"

"There's not a drop in the house, Dick."

"I forgot. Curse the luck!"

Just then a man entered the house only less brutal-looking than Dick himself.

He held a letter in his hand.

Dick seized it eagerly.

"It's from the father of the boy," he said.

The letter proved to contain fifty dollars.

"I send this in advance," said the writer. "When the boy is safely delivered into my hands a hundred and fifty more will be paid to the one who brings him, and no questions asked.

HERMAN FITCH."

"Good!" said Dick, "as far as it goes. I'm ready to give up the brat, but will his father keep faith? Perhaps he'll have the police on hand ready to nab me."

"Haven't you anybody to send—anybody you can trust?"

Dick slapped his knee forcibly. An idea had come to him.

"I'll send him in charge of the brat," he said, pointing to Jasper.

CHAPTER XXI.

JASPER IS INTRUSTED WITH A DELICATE COMMISSION.

"Look here, boy," said Dick, "do you want a job?"

"Yes," said Jasper, "if it's honest."

"No fear of that. I want you to take that boy home to his father."

"I'll do it," said Jasper, eagerly.

"How much pay do you want?"

"None at all, except money to pay my fare in the cars."

"You're the right sort," said Dick, with satisfaction. "But there's another matter I've got to think about. How do I know but you will betray me?"

"How?"

"Put the police on my track."

"If you hadn't given up the boy I might," said Jasper, frankly.

Dick regarded him attentively.

"You're bold," he said. "Then you won't betray me now."

"No."

"Promise it."

"I promise—that is, if you send the boy home by me."

"All right; that's understood. Now for another matter. Read that letter."

Jasper read the letter of Herman Fitch, already quoted.

"You see this man, the boy's father, agrees to pay one hundred and fifty dollars when he is given up."

"I see that."

"He will give you that money—that is, if he means fair—and you will bring it to me. Do you understand?"

"I do."

"Do you promise that?"

"I promise that, too. Where am I to find you? Here?"

"No; I'll give you an address in St. Louis."

"Does the father live in St. Louis?"

"He lives a little out of the city. His name is in the directory, so you won't have any trouble in finding it."

"How glad he will be to see the little boy again!"

"He ought to be. You don't think he'll back out from his agreement?" said Dick, suspiciously.

"No; he'll be so glad to see the child, he will care nothing for the money."

"That's what I hope. When I get that money I'm going East."

"You'll take me with you, Dick?" asked his wife.

"What good'll you be?" growled Dick. "It'll cost more."

"What can I do alone, here?"

"I'll leave money for your board."

"But I'll be so lonely, Dick," she persisted.

"Oh, I'll come back! It's business I'm going for, old woman. If I can't come back I'll send money to bring you."

"Do let me go with you, Dick."

"Oh, hush up! I can't have you always in my way. What, blubbering? Plague take all the women, I say!"

"When do you want me to go?" said Jasper.

"There's a train this afternoon; take that, for the sooner matters are arranged the better. Here's five dollars. It'll be more than enough to pay your fare, but you'd better have it in case anything happens."

Jasper felt some repugnance in taking money acquired in such a way, but it seemed necessary, and he thrust the note into his vest-pocket.

"You'll be able to carry the boy back to-night," said Dick. "To-morrow at twelve bring the money to this address."

He handed him a greasy-looking card with the name "Mark Mortimer, No. 132 S—— Street," scrawled on it in pencil.

"Am I to ask for Mark Mortimer?" asked Jasper.

"Yes, that's me—that is, it's one of my names. Don't fail."

"I won't."

"If you should play me false, you'd better never have been born," said the kidnapper, menacingly.

"I'll come, not on account of your threats, but because I have promised," said Jasper, quietly.

"You're a plucky boy. You ain't one of the milk-and-water sort," said Dick, with respect for the boy's courage.

"Thank you," said Jasper, laughing. "I am not often afraid."

"By Jove! you've got more pluck than half the men. You'd make a fine lad for my business."

"I don't think I'd like your business, so far as I know what it is," said Jasper.

"Well, there's some I'd like better myself. If my sister does the right thing by me I'll become a model citizen—run for Congress, may be. Eh, old woman?"

"I wish you would reform, Dick," said his wife.

"Let the world give me a chance, then. Now, boy, you must be starting."

"Harry," said Jasper to the little boy, whose name he had learned, "do you want to go with me?"

The little boy confidingly put his arms round our hero's neck.

"Will you take me to my mamma?" he asked.

"Yes, I will take you to her."

The little boy uttered a cry of delight.

"Me all ready!" he said, eagerly.

"Do you think he can walk to the depot?" asked Jasper.

"Yes; it is only a mile or so."

"Then I will start."

Part of the way he carried the little boy in his arms. They could make but slow progress, but luckily there was plenty of time, and they reached the depot a quarter of an hour before the train started.

The station-master looked at the two with curiosity.

"Is that boy yours?"

"He isn't my son, if that's what you mean," said Jasper, amused.

"Brother, then?"

"No; he's a friend of mine that I'm taking home to his father and mother."

"Been makin' a visit around here?" asked the station-master.

"Yes," replied Jasper, briefly.

The arrival of two passengers, who wanted tickets, relieved him from the questions of the curious station-master. He might have asked questions which it would have been inconvenient to answer.

"Did you ever ride in the cars, Harry?" asked Jasper.

"I did ride in the cars when the ugly man took me from my mamma."

"Was that the only time?"

The little boy could remember no other.

Jasper led him a little away, to avoid questioning, but was back in time to enter the cars when the train arrived. He found a vacant seat, and gave the little boy the place next the window. There were many admiring glances directed toward the little fellow, who was remarkably handsome. Jasper was apprehensive lest the boy should be recognized by some one who knew him. This would have brought suspicion upon him, and placed him in a very embarrassing position. Fortunately, though the child's appearance was much admired, no such recognition took place.

Two hours later they rolled into the central depot at St. Louis.

"Now," thought Jasper, "I must find out as soon as possible where Mr. Fitch lives."

Jasper had not been much of a traveller, as we know. Finding himself now in a strange city, he felt at first a little bewildered—the more so, that he had a young child under his charge. He did not know in which direction the boy's father lived, but the natural thought occurred to him that he could find his name in the directory. He went into a lager-beer saloon near-by and asked:

"Will you let me see your directory?"

"I got no directory," answered the burly Dutchman, who presided over the saloon. "I can give you lager."

"Not at present," said Jasper, laughing. "We don't drink."

It occurred to him that it might be as well to get into the central part of the city. He accordingly hailed a passing car, and got aboard with Harry.

After awhile he judged from the appearance of the buildings that he had reached one of the principal streets. He descended from the car, lifting Harry carefully down and carrying him in his arms to the sidewalk. There was a large and imposing store situated at the corner of the street.

"They must have a directory in there," thought Jasper.

He entered, holding the little boy by the hand. What was his surprise when a richly-dressed lady, turning and catching sight of the child, sprang to him, seized him in her arms, and began to cry and laugh alternately. But the mystery was explained when he heard Harry say:

"Oh, mamma, I am so glad to see you!"

CHAPTER XXII.

A BUSINESS MAN'S SUSPICIONS.

Jasper stood at a little distance, witnessing the happy meeting between the mother and child. He did not wish to interrupt their happiness. Soon, however, the mother looked up, and then Jasper advanced, raising his hat, politely.

"Is this Mrs. Fitch?" he asked.

"Yes," said the lady, surveying him with curiosity.

"Then I have great pleasure in restoring to you your child."

"What? Did he come with you?"

"Yes, madam."

"Did you know I was in here?"

"No; I only came in to consult the directory to learn your residence."

"How could you be so wicked as to steal my boy?" demanded Mrs. Fitch, with pardonable indignation, judging that Jasper was the kidnapper.

"I wouldn't have done it for five thousand dollars!" said Jasper, impetuously.

"He didn't 'teal me, mamma," said little Harry, coming opportunely to Jasper's defense.

"Who did, then, my darling?"

"It was big, ugly man. Jasper good boy—kind to Harry."

Mrs. Fitch, prompt to remedy her injustice, held out her hand to Jasper, which he took respectfully.

"Excuse me," she said; "but I thought, as Harry was with you, that you had been concerned in his kidnapping."

"I never saw him till this morning," said Jasper. "Chance drew me to a lonely house where he was confined."

"And you rescued him! How can I thank you?"

"I would have done so if I could, but I can't take the credit of it. Your husband offered a reward, which the kidnapper thought best to accept. He did not dare to bring him back himself, and having no one else to employ, asked me to become his agent in restoring him. Of course, I was very glad to do it."

"It was not chance that directed you to the haunt of these wicked men; it was a good and merciful Providence. Did they ill-treat my darling?"

"I found him tied to the bed in which he was lying."

"How could they treat you so my dear boy!" said the mother, piteously. "May I ask your name?"

This was, of course, addressed to Jasper.

"My name is Jasper Kent."

"Can you come out and stop at our house over night? We live about two miles distant. I want my husband to see you and thank you for bringing back our darling boy."

Jasper reflected that he must see Mr. Fitch, at any rate, in order to obtain the promised reward. Moreover, he had no means of his own to pay for a lodging, and he promptly accepted the offer.

"I will return home at once," said Mrs. Fitch. "I came in to make some purchases, but I can't think of those now. Come, Mr. Kent."

"Take hold of my hand," said little Harry to Jasper.

Jasper smilingly took the proffered hand, and Harry, happy in the double companionship, went out of the store.

There was a handsome carriage in waiting, with a coachman in livery perched on the box.

"Edward," said Mrs. Fitch, her face fairly glowing with delight, "do you see? Little Harry has come back."

"So he has, Heaven bless him!" said the coachman, heartily. "How do you do, Master Harry?"

"I'm pooty well," answered the little boy.

"Where did you find him, ma'am, if I may be so bold?"

"This young gentleman brought him back, Edward. Now, drive right home."

"Won't you go around to the office, ma'am, and tell master?"

"No; he must have left the office by this time. We shall see him at supper to-night."

Half an hour later the carriage drew up in front of a handsome residence, far enough from the centre of the city to have a side yard of considerable dimensions, in the rear of which stood a brick stable. It was clear that Mr. Fitch was a man of wealth, so Jasper decided.

Of the sensation produced in the house by Harry's arrival I will not speak. Jasper found himself regarded in the light of the heroic deliverer of the little boy from captivity, though he laughingly disclaimed the credit attaching to such a character.

They had been home but fifteen minutes when Mr. Fitch arrived. At the moment of his arrival Jasper was in a handsome chamber on the second floor, which had been assigned to his use, preparing himself for dinner. Mr. Fitch was overjoyed at the recovery of his little boy, but he listened with some incredulity to the praises lavished upon Jasper by his wife.

"You don't seem to realize," he said, "that this young hero of yours is a companion and acknowledged agent of a kidnapper."

"Wait till you see him," said Mrs. Fitch, confidently.

Mr. Fitch shrugged his shoulders.

"How the women are carried away by a specious appearance!" he thought. "I am a man of the world, and cooler in my judgment."

Yet when Jasper entered the room he could not help acknowledging that his appearance was very much in his favor. Frank and manly in his looks, he met Mr. Fitch with gentlemanly ease.

"You are the young gentleman who brought back my little boy, I believe," said the father.

"Yes, sir," said Jasper. "I occupy, for the time being, the office of agent of the man who kidnapped him."

"Who is this man?"

"I should be willing to tell you if I had not promised secrecy."

"Then," said Mr. Fitch, with slight suspicion, "you are in confidential relations with this villain."

"Partly so, but it was forced upon me. I never met him till to-day, and he confided in me because there seemed to be no one else that he could trust."

"Why did he not come himself?"

"Because he thought it would be dangerous."

"Shall you meet him again?"

"Once only, to finish this business. He said you had promised a certain sum on the boy's return, and this I agreed to carry him."

"How much commission are you to receive?" inquired Mr. Fitch.

"Nothing at all," said Jasper. "He handed me five dollars to pay the railroad fare of little Harry and myself to St. Louis. What is left over I shall return to him."

"Then Harry was not concealed in this city?"

"No, sir; but he was at no great distance from it."

"Are you living here?"

"I never was in St. Louis until this afternoon. I have only just come on from the State of New York."

"To find employment, I suppose?"

"Yes, sir. It was by the merest chance that I fell over your little boy and his captor. I was contriving plans for getting him away, when fortunately the kidnapper received a communication from you which led to my being here."

"Suppose you had got Harry away from this man, how could you have found me?"

"That would have been the difficulty. I didn't know your name, or where you lived. But I meant to come here and get one of the daily papers to publish an account of the recovery, in the hope that the paragraph would find its way to your notice."

"A very sensible plan," commented Mr. Fitch, approvingly. "When have you agreed to meet the kidnapper to carry him the money?"

"To-morrow at twelve."

"And then you will proceed to carry out your own plans?"

"Yes, sir. After supper, if you can spare the time, I will tell you my situation, and the circumstances that led me here, and ask for advice."

"Very well. I will gladly give you the best counsel I can."

After supper Jasper told his story briefly, and confirmed the favorable impression he had already begun to make. Mr. Fitch cast aside his lingering remnant of suspicion, and promised his good offices in procuring him employment.

"After you have seen this man and paid him the money," he said, "come to my counting-room, and we will talk over your affairs."

The evening was spent socially, little Harry, of course, being the central object of interest. The little fellow appeared to have taken a great fancy to Jasper, and was unwilling to have him go the next day. He was not reconciled till Jasper promised to come back.

CHAPTER XXIII.

WHERE JASPER FOUND DICK.

To find the address given by the kidnapper was not difficult. It was only necessary to look over a plan of the city, which Jasper did in Mr. Fitch's counting-room.

"Come back when your business is over," said the merchant.

"I will," said Jasper.

He set out with one hundred and fifty dollars in his pocket for 132 S—— Street.

We will precede him.

It was a shabby house of two stories, with a wide front. It looked dilapidated and neglected, but except that it was in an unsavory neighborhood there was nothing to draw attention to it, or lead to the impression that it was the haunt of lawbreakers and desperate characters.

In a back room sat three men, one of whom we recognize as the kidnapper, Dick, alias Mark Mortimer. Of the other two, one was under twenty-five, with a reckless, dare-devil look, as of one who would stop at little in his criminal schemes. He had more than once been engaged in burglary, but as yet had escaped detection.

The third was a stout, square-built man, of middle age, with a heavy, brutal face, such as might belong to a prize-fighter. He, too, was a burglar, an accomplished counterfeiter, a gambler, who supplemented luck by various swindling devices, in which he was an adept. This man was known as Slippery Bill, while his young companion was Jack, with a choice of last names.

The three men were playing a game of euchre, with a pack of greasy cards. The time was half-past eleven in the forenoon.

"It's most time for the boy to come," said Dick, looking toward the clock.

"How do you know but he'll give you the slip?" suggested Jack.

"If he did I'd break his neck!" exclaimed Dick, hastily. "But he won't. Leastways he won't if he can help it."

"It strikes me, Dick," said Bill, "that you ought never to have asked him to come here."

"Why not?"

"Who's to tell but he may bring company?" continued the stout man.

"What kind of company?"

"The police."

"He won't," said Dick.

"How do you know?"

"I'll trust him. He's a good 'un."

"How long have you known him, that you speak with so much confidence?" inquired the younger man.

"Since yesterday morning," answered Dick, cornered.

The two men burst into a boisterous laugh.

"Why, Dick, you're as innocent as a baby. You haven't knowed this chap more'n twenty-four hours, and you'll stake your life on him."

"Laugh as much as you like," said Dick, stubbornly. "I ought to speak up for my own nephew."

"Your nephew!" exclaimed his two companions, in surprise. "What do you mean?"

"What I say. He's my sister's son."

"A minute ago you said you never saw him till yesterday," said the stout man, suspiciously.

"No more I did. My sister lives at the East."

"Has she sent him to you to be brought up in the way he should go?" asked Jack, with a sneer.

"No; the boy's run away. He came across me by chance."

"That's better," said Bill, partially reassured. "He won't be likely to betray you—not now—but he may inform against this place."

"I'll answer for him."

"Are you going to let him go as soon as he brings the money, or will he stay with you?"

"Oh, he'll go. I can't take care of a lad like him. I've other fish to fry."

"Suppose we keep him and train him up to our business?"

"He ain't the right sort for that."

"Shows the white feather, eh?"

"No; he's as brave as any boy I ever saw."

"What's the matter, then?"

"He's too honest and virtuous."

"What! your nephew, Dick?" and the two men laughed loudly. "That's too thin. Don't ask us to swallow that."

"It's true."

"Why did he run away from home, then?"

"My sister's got a very rough temper—that's why."

"We can believe that," said Jack, "better than the other."

"Look here, Jack," said Dick, who was getting irritated, "you may find that I've got the same kind of temper if you keep on badgering me about the boy. I say he's to be trusted."

"He can be trusted under our eye. Have you any objection to our detaining him?"

"There's no need."

"I say there is. You've let him into the knowledge of this place. He'll blow on us some day."

"Do as you like," said Dick; "I don't care. I wash my hands of the responsibility."

"That's all we want," said Bill. "We need a young one to help us in our plans. If this nephew of yours is as brave as you say, he'll do. What time was he to come here?"

"Twelve."

"Then it's a minute past the time. I don't think he'll come."

"The clock may be wrong." said Dick, but he glanced uneasily at the clock, which now indicated a little past the hour.

His suspense was not a long one.

An old man, thin and shriveled, with a crafty eye, and a thin, squeaking voice, here put his head in at the door.

"Is Mr. Mark Mortimer here?" he asked.

"That's me!" exclaimed Dick, jumping up eagerly.

"There's a boy wants to see you, Mr. Mark Mortimer," said the old man, repeating the name as if he enjoyed it.

"It's my nephew," said Dick.

"Is his name Mortimer, too?" asked the proprietor of the establishment, for such the old man was.

"Never mind," said Dick, impatiently. "Bring the boy in."

Almost directly Jasper was ushered into the room—fearlessly, but looking about him with some curiosity.

The two men, who had not before seen him, surveyed him with equal curiosity.

"He does you credit," said the stout man.

"He's what I was at his age," said Dick. "Now, boy, have you got the money?"

"Yes," said Jasper.

"One hundred and fifty dollars?"

"Yes."

Dick's eyes glistened.

"Give it here. You're a trump. Did old Fitch make any difficulties?"

"No; he was glad to get the boy back."

"Did he ask you about me?"

"Yes."

"How much did you tell him?" demanded the kidnapper, hastily.

"Nothing. I told him that I had made a promise not to tell."

Dick looked triumphantly at his two companions.

"Didn't I tell you?" he said.

"You have the boy's word for it," said Jack, with a quiet sneer. "How did you find your way here, boy?"

"I looked at a map of the city," answered Jasper.

"Where?"

"In the office of Mr. Fitch."

"Where did you pass last night?"

"At the house of Mr. Fitch."

"Where are you going when you leave here?"

"I have promised to go to Mr. Fitch's counting-room."

"You seem to be very intimate with this gentleman," said Jack.

"There's nothing strange in that," said Jasper, quietly. "It was I who carried his boy home."

"The boy is right," said Dick, who, having obtained his money, felt graciously disposed toward our hero, through whose agency he had obtained it.

"What does he want of you?" asked Jack, continuing the cross-examination.

"I hope he is going to help me to a place," answered Jasper.

"No need of going to him," said the stout man. "We'll give you employment."

"You!" repeated Jasper, with an attentive glance, which took in the man's disreputable appearance.

"Yes, if you deserve it. What do you say?"

"I feel obliged for your offer," said Jasper, "but having promised Mr. Fitch to return, I would prefer to do so."

"Boys," interrupted Dick, at this point, "I'm sorry to leave this festive crowd, but I've got other business to attend to, and must be going."

"I'll go with you," said Jasper, who was anxious to leave the place.

"No, you don't, just yet," said Jack, rising, and striding between Jasper and the door. "We'll have a drink all around first."

"Thank you," said Jasper, "I don't drink."

"You must drink now. It's the law of this establishment."

"All right, Jasper," said Dick. "I'll treat. You can drink what you like, though."

Jasper felt that it would be politic to comply, and chose lemonade.

"I'll order the drinks," said Jack, and he left the room for that purpose.

CHAPTER XXIV.
THE SLEEPING POTION.

Presently the old man already referred to appeared with the drinks. It Is hardly necessary to say that Jasper was alone in his choice of lemonade. The rest selected stronger liquors.

"Here's to you, Dick," said Jack, tossing off the contents of his glass, "and may you live to treat us many times more!"

"Amen to that!" said Bill.

"Haven't you got anything to say, youngster?" asked Dick, turning to Jasper.

"I wish you a pleasant journey," said Jasper, politely.

"As to that, it depends on my success with my sister."

"When do you leave?"

"To-night, if I can."

"What's all that about, Dick? Are you going to leave us?" asked Bill.

"I'm goin' East for the benefit of my health and my purse," said Dick, with a grin. "Do you wish me success, mates?"

"To be sure. Is it anything we can help you in?"

"No, no. It's my private venture."

"Anything in my line?"

"No; it's a strictly virtuous and honest undertaking. I don't mind giving you a hint of it. I've got a near relative that's come into a fortune. Now I think I ought to come in for a share."

"To be sure!"

"Have another game of euchre, Dick?"

"I don't know—I ought to be going," said the kidnapper, hesitating. "We'll make it poker, and the boy may take a hand."

"No," said Jasper, languidly. "I don't know how to play."

"We'll teach you."

"I don't care about it."

"You look sleepy, lad," said Dick.

"Yes, I feel so. It's strange. I didn't feel so when I came in."

"Oh, don't mind the boy's looks," said Jack. "Lay down on that settee, if you want to, boy."

Jasper felt so heavy and drowsy that he accepted the permission and stretched himself out, closing his eyes.

"Why am I so sleepy?" he thought, languidly. "I never was before, in the middle of the day, except when I was sick."

He listened at first to the conversation between the players, but gradually it sounded only like a confused hum, and at length he could not hear it at all.

He was fast asleep.

When this became clear through his heavy breathing, Dick turned to the younger man, and pointing to Jasper, asked:

"What have you been doing to him?"

"I put a sleeping potion into his drink," answered Jack.

"What for?"

"I mean to keep him for a while, and that saves a fuss."

"What do you want to do with him?"

"Prevent him from doing mischief."

"There's no need. He can be trusted."

"You can trust him, for you'll be a long way off. He might blow on us any time."

Dick shrugged his shoulders.

"Oh, well, do as you please, but you're over careful. Don't hurt him."

"He'll be all right as long as he behaves himself. It's your deal."

The game was over at last, and Dick arose to go. Jasper was sleeping soundly, and was wholly unconscious of his departure.

"Give me a hand, Bill, and we'll take the boy up stairs," said the younger man.

"What's your plan, Jack?"

"To make him one of us. He'll come to it in time."

There was a windowless room on the second floor, in the centre of the house, wholly dark, except when lighted by gas. It was to this room that our hero was conveyed, and laid upon some bedding in the corner of the room. There was a slide in the partition to admit air, and with it a few faint rays of light. Jasper stirred a little while he was being moved, but the sleeping potion had too much potency to allow him to wake.

"There," said Jack, in a tone of satisfaction, "he's safe now."

"He'll make a fuss when he gets up."

"Let him. He can't get out."

As they went down stairs, Jack called aside Nathan Gibson, the old man who had charge of the house.

"Nathan," said he, "did you see the boy that was with us just now?"

"Yes."

"We've put him in the prison" (for this was the name by which the small dark room was known). "He's not to be let out."

"Good! I understand."

"You may take him some supper at five or six o'clock. Look in before that time to see if he's awake."

"All right!" said the old man, grinning. "What's your game?"

"It's your game as well as mine. The boy ought never to have come here. He may blow on us."

The mean-faced little man looked by turns frightened and fierce.

"I'd slit his throat if he did!" he said.

"No need of that. We'll make him join us."

"That would be the best way; but can you?"

"We can try. Don't forget what I told you."

Nathan nodded.

Still Jasper slept, little suspecting into what a trap he had walked.

CHAPTER XXV.

JASPER FINDS HIMSELF A PRISONER.

It was after five o'clock when Jasper opened his eyes. As soon as consciousness returned he looked around him with astonishment and wonder.

"Where am I?"

A few rays of light entered at the sliding-door above, and to this his eyes were naturally drawn.

Here was another puzzle. He explored his memory, and could recall no such place as this. He had never before been in such a room.

At last he recalled the circumstances under which he fell asleep, and he jumped to the conclusion that he was in the same house still.

"They must have put me to bed," he said to himself. "They were very kind; but this is a queer room."

Thus far no thought that he was a prisoner had entered his mind.

He arose and began to feel his way around by the walls. He judged that he was in a room not more than ten feet square. He could form no idea what was the time. It might be the middle of the night, so far as he knew.

"This is awkward," he thought. "I don't fancy being shut up like this. Where's the door? There must be one somewhere."

He found it at last, and tried the lock, but it did not yield to his efforts.

Then came the startling thought:

"Am I a prisoner?"

He stopped short and thought over the situation. He recalled all he could of the men in whose company he had been at the time he went to sleep. The longer he thought the more it seemed probable that it was as he suspected.

Though a little startled at this view of the situation, Jasper was by no means disposed to be despondent. His courage arose with the difficulties of his position.

"I'll find out how matters stand," he said to himself. "I'll pound till somebody comes."

He began to pound on the walls of the room with such effect that the old man below heard him.

"The bird is beating against the walls of his cage," he thought. "I'll go up and see him."

Presently Jasper heard steps ascending the stairs. Almost immediately another sliding-door about four feet from the floor was drawn open, and the old man's face was poked in.

"Did you knock?" he asked, grinning.

"Yes," said Jasper. "Open the door, and let me out."

"Won't you have some supper first?" asked Nathan, with a leer.

"No; I'd rather go out," said Jasper, in a tone of suspicion.

"I couldn't allow that. Oh, no!" said Nathan.

"What right have you to keep me here against my will?" exclaimed Jasper, furiously.

"We like your company so much, my dear young man," said Nathan, nodding his head waggishly.

"Who's 'we'?" demanded Jasper.

"Jack, and Bill, and me."

"Let me out, I say."

"Don't be agitated, my dear boy. You'll be taken good care of."

"I'd rather take care of myself. Will you open the door?"

"I couldn't, but I'll bring you up some supper directly."

The sliding-door was closed suddenly, and again Jasper found himself in the dark, fully understanding now that he was a prisoner, but why, he could not form a conjecture.

CHAPTER XXVI.
IN CONFINEMENT.

Soon the old man reappeared and opened the sliding-door. He carried a small waiter containing a cup of tea, a plate of cold meat, and a slice of white bread without butter.

"We don't want you to starve," he said. "Here's something to stay your stomach. You're hungry, ain't you?"

Jasper admitted that he was.

"I thought so. When I was your age I was always eating. Never could get enough."

Jasper wondered, if this were the case, why the old man had not grown larger, but he did not say this. He took the waiter from Nathan and set it on his lap, there being no table.

"I hope you don't mean to keep me long as a boarder," he said. "You won't find it profitable, boarding me for nothing."

"That isn't for me to say," said Nathan. "Jack and Bill will see to that."

"Did they tell you to confine me?"

"Yes; I told you that already."

"Will you ask them to come up and speak to me? I want to know why I am here."

"They ain't at home now. I'll tell them when they come in."

"Thank you. Do you think that will be to-night?"

"Not likely. They'll come in so late you'll be abed and asleep."

"Don't let them go out to-morrow morning without seeing me."

"I'll tell them."

The old man waited till Jasper had finished eating, and then took the waiter back through the window.

"Won't you let me have a light?" asked Jasper. "I don't want to stay here in the dark."

"You'll set the house on fire," said the old man, hesitating.

"And get burned up myself? I should be fool to run such a risk as that."

This consideration suggested itself to the old man's judgment, and he promised to bring up a lamp before long.

This he really did. Jasper found it a great relief. He was now broad awake, the effect of the drug having passed off.

There was nothing to do, indeed, but his thoughts were busy, and he tried hard to devise some method of escape, in case he should not be released.

The next morning breakfast was brought to him about eight o'clock. It was not till ten that the sliding-door was opened and the face of Jack appeared at the opening.

"Well, boy, how do you like your quarters?" he asked, with a disagreeable smile.

"Not at all," answered Jasper. "Why do you keep me here?"

"We had reasons for putting you here."

"What were they?"

"First and foremost, you knew too much."

"Were you afraid I should betray you?" asked Jasper.

"You might."

"I promise not to, if you will let me go."

"That's all very well, but when you get out you might break your promise."

"Then it would be for the first time," said Jasper, proudly. "I never break my promises."

"You talk well, boy, but it's easy to talk."

"It's all I can do. There is no way of proving what I say."

"That's so; and that's the reason I'm going to keep you."

"At that rate, you will have to keep me all my life."

"No; there's another way."

"What is it?" asked Jasper, eagerly.

"Join us, and when you're in the same box you won't go to blabbing."

"What do you mean by joining you?" asked Jasper, though he was afraid he understood only too well.

"You ought to be smart enough to know that."

"I don't know what your business is," said our hero.

"You don't!" said Jack, ironically. "Perhaps you think we're commission merchants, or bankers, or something of that kind, Bill and me?"

"I don't think you are either of them," said Jasper, laughing.

"Why not?"

"You don't look like a commission merchant or a banker."

"What do I look like, eh, boy?"

"You may be angry if I answer that question."

"No, I won't. Go ahead!"

"You look as if you didn't get your living in any way so honest as that."

"Well, suppose you are right?"

"Then I am sorry. I wish you would reform and lead a different life."

"No preaching! I didn't bargain for that."

"Then all I have to say is, you are in no danger from me. I shall not betray you."

"Perhaps you are to be trusted, but I can't run the risk. You must join us."

"You may be wicked yourself. You have no right to make me so," said Jasper, firmly.

"That's all nonsense. The world owes me a living, and you, too."

"Not without work. I'm going to work for my living."

"I mean you shall. You shall work for me."

"That kind of work will do the world no good. I want to do something useful."

"So you shall. You shall help us bleed some of these bloated aristocrats. They've got more money than is good for them—more than they have any business to keep."

"I don't agree with you," said Jasper.

"You'd better. It is for your interest," said Jack, frowning.

"It can't be for my interest to become a law-breaker."

"Then you can stay here till you rot!" retorted the burglar, roughly. "You won't come out of this chamber till you have agreed to become one of us."

There was something in this threat which startled Jasper, bold and brave as he was.

"Such an outrage won't be permitted," he said.

"Won't it?" sneered Jack. "We'll see about that. I'll take the risk. You don't know me yet," he added, with an oath.

"Is it wholly because you are afraid I will betray you that you treat me in this way?" asked Jasper.

"No."

"What other reason have you?"

"I'll tell you. You're the sort of boy we want. You ain't any whining, milk-and-water sort of boy. You're brave and spirited. You would be worth a good deal to us."

Burglar though Jack was, Jasper was not insensible to the compliment. Any boy likes to be considered spirited, even if he does not deserve it, and he felt flattered by this tribute, which he felt that he deserved, at least, in part.

"I am glad you have a good opinion of my courage," he said, "but I think I can find a better use for it than in the career you open to me. If I accepted your proposal from fear of imprisonment it would show that I was not such a boy as you describe."

"You are an obstinate fool!" said Jack, with a frown.

"I am obstinate in this," said Jasper, composedly. "You want to spoil my life by making me a criminal."

"Do you mean to call me a criminal!" exclaimed Jack, angrily.

"I call you nothing—I only take you at your word."

"You'll talk differently from this a week from now!" said Jack, prepariug to shut the sliding-door.

"Do you mean to keep me in this dark hole a week?" asked Jasper, unable to repress a shudder.

"Ha! that disturbs you, does it?" asked the other, smiling sardonically.

"Yes, it does. You don't think I fancy it, do you?"

"Well, you know the way to end your imprisonment."

"Is there only one way?"

"There's only one way. Tell the old man, Nathan, when you've made up your mind to accept my offer."

Without waiting for a reply Jack pushed the sliding-door in its place, and once more Jasper found himself in the dark.

CHAPTER XXVII.

AN UNEXPECTED FRIEND.

Three days and nights passed, and Jasper was still in confinement. Three times a day Nathan came to bring him his meals. Each time he asked our hero:

"Are you ready to join our friends?"

And each time Jasper answered:

"No!"

"You must like staying here," said the old man.

"I am very tired of it," said Jasper, with a sigh.

"You can come out any time," said Nathan.

"Let me out now, then."

"Oh, no, my dear young friend," said Nathan, shaking his head, "not until you accept Jack's offer."

"Good heavens!" thought Jasper, "can it be possible that in the middle of a great city I can be imprisoned like this, with hundreds passing the house every hour? I wish I could be heard outside."

But this was impossible, owing to the peculiar situation of the room. The prospects of our young hero were certainly gloomy enough. But there's an old saying that the darkest hour is just before the dawn, and deliverance was nearer than Jasper supposed.

On the fourth day, at noon, Jasper heard steps ascending the stairs. He supposed it to be the old man, with his dinner, and he looked up listlessly as the sliding-door was opened. But instead of the wrinkled face of Nathan he beheld the fresh face of a young girl, apparently about sixteen years of age. She regarded the prisoner with curiosity and surprise.

"Here's your dinner," she said.

"Thank you," said Jasper. "Where is the old man that generally comes up?"

"Uncle Nathan? Oh, he's gone out for a little while."

"He's your uncle, then?"

"Yes."

"Do you live here?"

"I've only just come. He sent for me. What do they keep you here for?" she asked, her face expressing curiosity. "Are you sick?"

"I'm sick of being cooped up here."

"Then why do you stay?"

"Because I have to. Your uncle won't let me out."

"Why not?"

"Hasn't he told you?"

"No. He only told me to bring up your dinner. I thought it was a man. I didn't know it was a boy."

"You want to know why I am confined here?"

"Yes, if you'll tell me."

"It is because your uncle is afraid I'll inform the police against him and the men who come here."

"I don't know much about them. Are they bad people, then?"

"I am afraid they are. They do things that make them liable to be arrested."

"What! my uncle, too?" asked the girl, who appeared to be startled.

"I am not sure about him, but I feel sure about two men who come here. Their names are Jack and Bill."

"I know. I have seen them both. One is a young man, the other must be near fifty. He's stout."

"Yes."

"How long do you think they will keep you here?"

"Until I agree to join them in breaking the laws."

"That's too bad," said the girl, compassionately. "Isn't it awful to be shut up there?"

"Yes, it is. I've been here three or four days, and it seems as many weeks. Don't you think you could help me to escape?" asked Jasper, in a lower tone.

The girl looked frightened.

"I wouldn't dare to," she said.

"Wouldn't you, if you were sure your uncle wouldn't find out?"

"Yes, I would," she answered, heartily.

"Don't you think you could manage it?" asked Jasper, eagerly.

"I don't know. I wish I could," she answered, with evident sincerity.

"Nancy!" called the old man's voice from below, sharply, "hasn't that boy got through yet?"

"Coming, uncle," she answered.

"I'll speak with you again when I bring up your supper," she said, as she hurried down stairs.

She left Jasper eager and excited. At last he had made a friend in the camp of his enemies, and there was hope ahead.

CHAPTER XXVIII.

ESCAPE.

Jasper waited impatiently for supper-time, not that he was hungry, for excitement had taken away his appetite, but because he was feverish with anxiety as to his prospects of release.

"Suppose the old man should suspect her and come up with the supper himself," he thought, anxiously.

But his anxiety proved groundless.

A little after five the door was opened and disclosed the young girl, Nancy. His face lighted up joyfully.

"I'm glad it's you, Nancy," he said. "I was afraid I should see your uncle. Does he suspect anything?"

"No; he scolded me for allowing you so long to eat your dinner, that's all."

"I'll take it off the plate and eat afterward. Now, I want to talk a little. Have you found out any way to help me?"

"I don't know. Do you think you could get out of this window?"

Jasper looked at the aperture critically.

"Yes, I think I could," he said, after a pause, "with some one on the other side to pull me through."

"I'll do that," said Nancy.

"You will? You're a trump! What am I to do afterward? Can you help me to leave the house?"

"That's what I've been thinking," said Nancy. "I'm afraid it wouldn't do to let you out at the front door. It's locked and bolted, and the bolt squeaks. I've tried it to see."

"The windows?" suggested Jasper, anxiously.

"No, I am afraid not."

"Then if I can't leave the house, it's no use to get out of this room."

"Yes, there's another way out, but it requires courage."

"I'm not a coward," said Jasper.

"No, you don't look like it," said Nancy, who was more favorably disposed toward Jasper on account of his good looks.

"Thank you," said Jasper, gratified. "Now tell me, what is your plan?"

"There's a scuttle through which you can get out on the roof. Would you dare to do it?"

"Yes; I might get on to some other roof."

"Yes, but you might slip off."

"I am not afraid. You think of that because you are a girl."

"Yes. I would rather stay here than trust myself on the roof."

"Do you know if the next house is higher than this?"

"Yes, it is."

"That's very awkward," said Jasper, thoughtfully.

"But there are some windows in the side of the house. You might get in at one of them."

"And be taken for a house-breaker? Well, I must run the risk, any way. When do you think I had better try it?"

"To-night. There'll be nobody in the house to-night but uncle and me."

"That's good," said Jasper, reflecting that Nathan looked feeble, and being small in size would not be more than a match for his strength if the worst came to the worst.

"When does your uncle go to bed?" he asked.

"At eleven."

"When will you come for me?"

"At twelve, or a little after."

"Are the nights dark now?" asked Jasper. "It would be rather ticklish being on the roof if it were pitch dark."

"No, the moon will be up then."

"That's all right. If you find out anything else that will help, let me know."

"Yes, I will."

"Nancy!"

"Yes, uncle!" answered the girl. "To-night at twelve!" she said, in a low voice, and hurried down stairs.

Jasper, in thinking over the plan he had in view, realized that it was one that would probably require all his courage and nerve. It would be a great relief to get through without accident. But he never thought of backing out. He felt that anything was better than to be confined longer in his present prison.

It seemed a long time to wait, especially in the darkness, for the oil was burned out in his lamp, and there was no chance of asking for a further supply. He had forgotten it when Nancy came up with his supper. However, he felt that it was of no particular consequence, as he was so soon to be released.

So the hours passed. He did not permit himself to fall asleep, lest he should not be awake when Nancy came.

At last he heard a faint noise at the door, and saw Nancy standing outside with a candle.

"Are you ready?" she whispered.

"Yes, ready and waiting."

"Now try to get through, and I will help you."

She set down the candle, and Jasper set about his task. It was a tight squeeze, but at last he got out, and stood on his feet in the entry.

"Now, follow me," said Nancy, in a whisper.

He climbed a narrow, steep staircase, and then a ladder, and unfastening the scuttle, he laid it back. The moon shone softly down, bathing the city in its beautiful light. He got out lightly on the roof.

"Good-bye!" he said, "and thank you, Nancy."

"Good luck!" said Nancy.

He lowered the scuttle, and sat astride the roof, considering what to do next.

CHAPTER XXIX.

JASPER IN A NEW CHARACTER.

It was a relief to be out of his prison, but it must be admitted that Jasper's situation was not particularly desirable or agreeable. It was midnight, and he was seated astride the roof of the house which had served as his prison. There seemed to be no chance to reach the street, except to slide down the roof, and that would be certain death.

Jasper looked about him in great perplexity.

As his deliverer had told him, the next house was a story higher than the one on whose roof he was seated, and, still more important, there was a side-window looking out in that direction. When Jasper saw this, hope sprang up in his heart.

"If that window is not fastened I can get in," he thought.

He edged his way along to the window, and found that to reach it he would have to slide down a little way and catch hold of the blind to prevent sliding too far.

"There's some risk about it," thought Jasper. "Shall I try it?"

I don't know whether Jasper was justified in taking the risk he did, for there was great danger of sliding over into the street. I don't think I should have ventured to do it; but our hero was fearless and courageous, and he resolved that, as this was the only method of escape, he would avail himself of it. As a precaution against slipping, however, he took off his shoes, and catching the strings in his teeth commenced the perilous descent. He succeeded in grasping the blind and staying his progress.

"Now, if the window should be fastened, what should I do?" he thought.

But it was not. He succeeded in raising it, and with a feeling of intense relief made his way into the chamber.

Then for the first time there flashed upon him the thought that he had placed himself in a very suspicious predicament. He had entered a house at midnight through the window. Why might he not be taken for a burglar? This was the way a burglar was likely to enter, and if he should be caught here his explanation would be considered very unsatisfactory.

Jasper, brave as he was, was startled by this thought, while simultaneously the difficulty of escape was forced upon him. He looked about him in mental disturbance.

It was a small attic chamber. There was a bed in the room, a wash-stand, a couple of chairs, and a clothes-press. This, being open, revealed a few clothes belonging, apparently, to a man.

"Why isn't he here?" thought Jasper, "and what shall I do if he comes?"

Though his story was true, he nevertheless felt that it was improbable, and before he could tell it he thought it likely that an alarm would be given, resulting in his being consigned to the care of the police.

An idea came to him.

He opened the bed, drew out one of the sheets and arrayed himself in it, after carefully folding back the quilt.

"Now," he said to himself, "if it is necessary, I will see what sort of a ghost I can make."

Hardly had he done this than he heard steps ascending the stairs. Jasper had little doubt that it was the occupant of the chamber which he had so unceremoniously entered.

"I'll get into the wardrobe if I can," he thought.

He managed to squeeze himself into the wardrobe, and waited with anxiety for the arrival of the new-comer.

Through a crevice he saw the entrance of a stout, good-natured-looking young man, whistling a popular song. He was probably a clerk or young mechanic, who, after a hard day's work, had been to some cheap place of amusement. Wholly unconscious of Jasper's presence, the young man undressed himself, still continuing to whistle, and got into bed. It was so light outside that he had not lighted the gas.

"I wonder how long it'll take for him to get to sleep?" thought Jasper. "I'm getting tired of being cooped up here."

Unfortunately for him the young man seemed to be in no hurry. He whistled to himself, and occasionally sung in a low tone. At length Jasper decided to make a desperate move. Observing that the young man was lying with his face turned from the wardrobe, he seized his opportunity, stepped softly out, and gained the middle of the floor before he was seen.

The effect upon the young man was startling. The whistle died away, and with blanched cheeks and staring eyes he sat bolt upright in bed.

"Oh, Lord!" he exclaimed, tremulously. "What are you?"

Not a word escaped from the white figure, but it solemnly waved its hand.

"Are you a ghost?" asked the young man.

Jasper made a guttural noise and waved his arm again.

"Oh, Lord preserve me!" ejaculated the young man, shaking with terror. "Go away, do, good ghost! I haven't done anything!"

As he spoke he covered up his head with the bedclothes, and Jasper could see by the convulsive movements that he was in a state of the greatest agitation. Our hero felt inclined to laugh, but forebore. He considered whether it would be safe, disguised as he was, to make his way down stairs and out at the front door. But another course suddenly suggested itself. The young man looked good-natured. Why shouldn't he reveal himself to him, and throw himself upon him for protection? Besides, he was sorry to frighten him so much.

Acting upon his new resolution, he threw off the sheet and said in his natural voice:

"Don't be frightened. I am not a ghost."

The young man in bed took courage to uncover his head.

"Ain't you a spirit?" he said, doubtfully.

"No more than you," said Jasper, laughing.

"What made you frighten me so? Who are you?"

"I am a friend of yours."

"I don't think I ever saw you before. How did you get in?"

"Through the window."

"You ain't a burglar, are you?" asked the young man, with fresh apprehension.

"Of course not," said Jasper, laughing. "Do I look like a burglar?"

"No; but I don't see what made you come in."

"The fact is, I want you to help me," said Jasper. "Just light the gas, and I'll tell you all about it."

He spoke so frankly and straightforwardly that the young man was reassured. He got out of bed and lighted the gas.

"There! do I look like a burglar?" asked Jasper.

"No, you don't; but I don't see how you got in."

"Then I'll tell you. I've just escaped from the next house."

"Escaped?"

"Yes. I was locked up in a dark room for four days, and the only way I could get out was through the roof. Of course I couldn't slide off into the street and break my neck, so I got in here through the window."

"You don't say!" ejaculated the young man. "What did they shut you up for? Was it your father?"

"No. It's a long story. I knew something they were afraid I would tell."

"What are you going to do?"

"I am going to ask you to let me out into the street."

"What! so late as this? You would have to stay out all night."

"That would be better than to be locked up as I have been for the last four days."

"Suppose you wait till morning. This bed is big enough for both of us."

"Thank you. I should like that, and shall be much obliged to you."

"You are sure you are not a burglar?" said the young man, with a brief return of his former suspicion.

"Neither burglar nor ghost," said Jasper.

"What made you put on the sheet?"

"I was afraid you would take me for a burglar, so I meant to frighten you and escape, concluding that you would be afraid to pursue me."

"That's so. I really thought you were a spirit."

"If you think so now, just feel my muscle," said Jasper, smiling.

"I don't think so now."

"If I am to sleep with you, here is your sheet. We can make better use of it than in masquerading as ghosts."

Jasper undressed himself and got into bed. He learned that his companion's name was Adam Diedrich, and that he kept a small cigar store near-by.

CHAPTER XXX.

JASPER GETS A PLACE.

Jasper took breakfast the next morning with the friendly young German, whose acquaintance he had so singularly made. Not a word was said as to the manner in which he had entered the house. He was introduced by Adam as "my friend, Mr. Kent."

After breakfast Jasper went around with his new friend to the place of business of the latter. He decided not to call upon Mr. Fitch till about ten o'clock.

While on his way to the merchant's counting-room he met the girl, Nancy, with a tin pail in her hand. The girl's face lighted up when she saw him.

"So you got off the roof," she said. "I was so afraid you would fall."

"Thank you, Nancy," said Jasper. "Thanks to you I am out of prison."

"But how did you get off the roof?"

Jasper gave her an account of his midnight adventures.

"And now tell me," he said, "how does your uncle take my flight?"

"He's awful mad about it," said the girl, shaking her head.

"What does he think? Does he suspect you?" asked Jasper, eagerly.

"He did at first, but he doesn't now. He's puzzled to know how you got away. And Jack, he's mad, too."

"Jack, does he know it?"

"Yes; he came around to the house about eight o'clock. He was looking seedy, as if he'd been up all night. As near as I can find out, he failed in some job last night, and that made him cross."

"Very likely."

"'Have you carried up that boy's breakfast?' I heard him say.

"'No,' said my uncle.

"'Then give it to me, and I'll take it up; I want to talk to him.'

"So Uncle Nathan made me get the breakfast ready. I gave it to him, and he went up. A minute after he roared down stairs:

"'Where's the boy? What have you done with him?'

"Uncle Nathan stared, and called out:

"'Where's your eyes, Jack? Can't you see straight this morning?'

"Jack answered, as mad as could be:

"'Come up here, you old fool, and see if your eyes are any better than mine!'

"Uncle went up the stairs, two at a time, and looked in the chamber, too.

"'There, what do you say to that?' I heard Jack say.

"'I'm dumfounded!' said Uncle Nathan; and then he called me."

"Were you frightened?" asked Jasper.

"A little," said the girl. "I was afraid I'd look guilty.

"'Do you know anything about this?' asked my uncle, sternly.

"'Good gracious! You don't mean to say he's gone?' I said, looking as much surprised as possible. 'How did he get out?'

"'That's what I want to know,' said Jack, and he looked suspiciously at Uncle Nathan and me.

"'I'm as innocent as a new-born babe,' said Uncle Nathan.

"'Somebody must have let him out,' said Jack.

"'I guess he squeezed through the opening,' said I.

"'Maybe he did,' said Uncle Nathan.

"'Suppose he did, you'd see him or hear him. He couldn't get out.'

"'He might have got out through the door in the night,' said Uncle Nathan.

"'Did you find the door unlocked?' asked Jack.

"'Nancy was up first. How was it, Nancy?' asked my uncle.

"'No; it was all right,' said I.

"That puzzled them both. Then they thought of the roof, and went up. I was afraid they would find you there, but they didn't. They seemed to think you couldn't get away so, and they're dreadfully puzzled to know how you did escape. I was afraid you'd fallen off, so I went outside to see if I could find any blood on the sidewalk, but I couldn't, and I hoped you'd got into the next house."

"Your uncle didn't think of that, did he?"

"No, nor Jack, either."

"Well, I've been lucky. I only hope they won't suspect you."

"They will if they should see me talking to you in the street."

"Then we'd better separate. Good-morning, Nancy. I won't forget the service you've done me."

"Good-morning, Jasper. I'm so glad you got away."

"I wish you were away, too, Nancy. It's not a good place for you."

"I don't think I shall stay long," said the girl. "I didn't know uncle kept such company or I wouldn't have come to his house. Some day I shall leave him, and then I shall go out to service."

"That would be better for you. I advise you to do it soon."

The two parted company, and Jasper proceeded at once to Mr. Fitch's office.

"I wonder what he'll think of me?" Jasper said to himself. "I promised to come back after carrying the money, and now it is four days late."

"Is Mr. Fitch in the counting-room?" asked our hero of the clerk.

"Yes, but he's busy."

"I will wait, then."

"Can't I attend to your business?"

"I think not."

"Your business must be very important," said the clerk, with a sneer.

"I don't know about that," said Jasper, composedly, "but I think if you will tell Mr. Fitch that Jasper Kent is here he will receive me."

"Is your name of such weight?" asked the clerk, with another sneer.

"Suppose you put it to the test," said Jasper, smiling.

The clerk had not seen Jasper when he called before and didn't recognize him as the restorer of little Harry; otherwise, he would have treated our hero with more attention.

Influenced by curiosity he went into the counting-room and announced Jasper's name.

"Bring him in," said the merchant.

Jasper entered, but the manner of Mr. Fitch differed greatly from what it had been when they parted four days before. Then it was cordial and friendly, now it was cold and suspicious.

"Good-morning, Mr. Fitch," said Jasper.

"Good-morning," responded the merchant, coldly. "You have been a long time returning from your errand!"

"That's true, sir; but I would have come sooner if I could."

Mr. Fitch looked up in surprise.

"Do you mean to say that you couldn't come?" demanded he.

"Yes, sir."

"What prevented you?"

"I was in close confinement."

"What! were you arrested?" and again the merchant's face was overspread by doubt and suspicion.

"No, sir; I hope I shall never fall into the hands of the police."

"How then could you be in confinement? This is a riddle."

"The house to which I was requested to bring the money was a haunt of desperate men—burglars, I found out—and they were afraid I would betray their rendezvous. They mixed me some lemonade, which I now think must have been drugged, for I went to sleep in the middle of the day, soon after drinking it. When I awoke up I found myself in a dark room, in the centre of the house."

"Is this true?" asked the merchant, amazed. "Can such things take place within earshot of the police?"

"Yes, sir; there was no chance of my making myself heard; if there had been I would have called for help."

"How did you get out, and when?"

"Last night, at midnight."

"How?"

"I will tell you, sir. That, I think, is the most interesting part of it."

"Proceed."

When Mr. Fitch had heard Jasper's explanation he no longer doubted him. His friendly, cordial manner returned, and he congratulated our hero on his prompt rejection of Jack's offers, though that rejection exposed him to continued imprisonment.

"Now," he asked, "what are your plans?"

"To get something to do," said Jasper.

"Of what kind?"

"Any kind."

"I will engage you, for the present, at ten dollars a week. Will that suit you?"

"Yes, sir. Nothing could suit me better."

"Do you think you can live on that?"

"Easily."

"Then that is settled. To-night you will go home with me. To-morrow will be soon enough to look for a boarding-place. Here are your first week's wages in advance."

"Thank you, sir. You are very kind."

"I have not forgotten that I am indebted to you for the recovery of my little Harry. Here, Leonard."

The clerk already mentioned entered the counting-room. He looked inquiringly from Jasper to Mr. Fitch.

"Leonard," said the latter, "this young man is to be your fellow-clerk. He takes the place of Victor, who left last week. Instruct him in his duties."

"Yes, sir," said the clerk, in no little surprise.

Jasper followed him out into the warehouse.

CHAPTER XXXI.

THE UNWELCOME RELATIVE.

Now that Jasper has found a place we can venture to leave him for a time and go back to the home which he had felt compelled to leave.

His step-mother felt relieved by his departure. It left her mistress of the situation, with no one to interfere with or question her authority. How Jasper fared she cared little, or not at all. How he was likely to get along without money she never inquired, nor did she feel a twinge of remorse for her treatment of one who had been her late husband's sole care and hope. It was enough for her that she had Nicholas with her. Stern as she generally was toward him, she was weakly indulgent. Whatever he wanted she gave him, if it were not utterly unreasonable. She was afraid he would tire of the country and want to go away, and this led her to gratify him in his wishes, in order that she might retain him at her side.

Nicholas was not slow in finding out his power and in using it. He asked and obtained a horse for his own use, and later an elegant little carriage was ordered from the city, in which he used to drive around the neighborhood with the airs of a young prince. To others he might seem arrogant and conceited— to his mother he was only possessed of the proper spirit of a gentleman. In her eyes he was handsome, though in the eyes of no one else.

But perfect happiness is short-lived. In her new prosperity Mrs. Kent forgot that she had a brother who was not likely to reflect credit upon the family. She had not heard from him for years, and supposed he did not know where she was. But in this, as we know, she was mistaken.

One day Nicholas was standing on the lawn in front of the house, waiting for his carriage to be brought around from the stable, when his attention was drawn to a common-looking man who was standing by the fence and looking at him in what he considered an impudently familiar way.

Since Nicholas had become a young aristocrat he was easily made angry by such familiarity on the part of anyone of the lower orders, and he resented it at once.

"Why are you standing there, fellow?" he demanded, frowning.

The man neither seemed overawed nor angry. He only looked amused.

"Because I am tired of walking," he said.

"Then go somewhere else."

"Thank you, this suits me very well," said the man, smiling provokingly.

"It doesn't suit me, though," said Nicholas, bristling up.

"Who are you?" inquired Dick, for it was he, with provoking nonchalance.

"Who am I? I'll let you know!" retorted Nicholas, now very angry.

"I wish you would. That's what I just asked you."

"I'm the owner of this place, and I warn you off."

"Oh, you're the owner of this place!" said the stranger, laughing. "Do you own the road, too?"

"Yes," said Nicholas, "I own the road in front of my place."

Dick laughed again.

"You're a young man, ain't you, to be a landed proprietor. How about your mother? Doesn't she own anything?"

"What do you know about my mother?" demanded Nicholas, a little nonplussed.

"More than you think for, young man," said Dick. "She used to go to school with me."

"Did she? Well, I suppose she couldn't help it if there were low persons in the school with her."

"That's good!" said the stranger, laughing heartily. "So I am a low person, am I?"

"You look like it," said Nicholas, insolently.

He expected the man would be angry, but instead he laughed more heartily than before.

Nicholas began to think he was crazy.

"Well, boy," he said, after a pause, "just remember that appearances are sometimes deceitful."

"I don't think they are so in this case," said Nicholas, "but I can't waste anymore time with you. There's my horse coming around. I'm going to ride."

"Is that your team? It's very neat, 'pon my word."

"That's nothing to you."

"Won't you give me a seat? I've never been in this town before, and I should like to take a drive."

"Look here, fellow, you've got cheek!" exclaimed Nicholas.

"Have I?"

"Do you think I would be seen in such low company?"

"Why not? I'm a gentleman. If you are a gentleman, then I am, too."

"What do you mean? What have I to do with you?"

"A good deal," said the stranger. "I am your uncle!"

Nicholas gasped for breath. What! this low, common person his uncle? He would not credit it.

"That's a lie!" he said. "You are trying to humbug me."

"Not so fast, nephew Nicholas," said Dick. "You can't alter facts. I'm your mother's brother. Didn't she ever tell you of your Uncle Dick?"

Uncle Dick! Nicholas did remember that his mother had named such a person, and the uncomfortable apprehension dawned upon him that the stranger's claim was well founded, after all. He kept silent, but flared at the stranger in a state of mental disturbance.

"I see you've heard of me," said Dick, with a short laugh. "Is your mother at home?"

"I believe so," said Nicholas, sullenly.

"I've come a long way to see her. Will you go in and tell her I am here?"

Nicholas was not overwilling to obey the person whom he had just called low, but he felt considerable curiosity as to whether the man was really his uncle, and this decided him to comply with his request.

"I will speak to my mother," he said. "She will know whether you are what you claim to be."

"Yes, she will know. I don't believe she has forgotten brother Dick."

Nicholas sought and found his mother.

"What, Nicholas, back so soon?" she said, looking up from her sewing.

"No, mother, I haven't started yet. There's a person down stairs who says he is my Uncle Dick, and he wants to see you."

"Good heavens! is he here?" exclaimed Mrs. Kent, in a tone of vexation. "How in the world did he find me out?"

"Then it is he? He is a very common-looking person."

"He's kept low associates. Where is he?"

"Down on the lawn."

"Tell him to come in. I suppose I shall have to see him."

"It may not be your brother after all," said Nicholas.

"I am afraid it is. I can tell soon as I see him."

Nicholas went down stairs in no very pleasant mood.

"You're to come in," he said, ungraciously. "My mother will see you."

"I thought so," said Dick, smiling complacently.

CHAPTER XXXII.

A COLD RECEPTION.

Richard Varley followed Nicholas into the presence of Mrs. Kent. The latter looked scrutinizingly at him as he approached, hoping that it might be an impostor. But, no! there was no mistaking his appearance. It was, indeed, her brother.

"How d'ye do, Helen," said Dick, with ostentatious cordiality.

"Very well, Richard," she answered coldly, slipping her hand out of his grasp as quickly as she could.

"The old girl ain't very glad to see me," thought Dick. "Just as I thought."

"How did you find me out?" asked Mrs. Kent.

"There was a man from this way told me of your good luck."

"Where were you, then?"

"In Missouri, near St. Louis."

"Indeed? Have you just come from there?"

"Yes."

"Did you have any business this way? I suppose you must, or you wouldn't have come so far."

"I came on purpose to see you, Helen," said Dick, trying to look like an affectionate brother, and signally failing.

"You are certainly very kind," said Mrs. Kent in a cold tone, evincing not the slightest pleasure at his devotion. "I am afraid you must have put yourself to a good deal of inconvenience on my account."

"Why, yes, I have," answered her brother, perceiving at once that he might urge this as a claim upon her; "but what of that? Ain't you my only sister, and hasn't it been years since we met?"

"Really, Richard," said Mrs. Kent, with a little quiet sarcasm, "I was hardly prepared to expect from you so great an interest in me. I wonder you didn't come before. It's a good many years since we met."

"Well, Helen, you see I couldn't afford it before. I wanted to see you, but I couldn't raise the money to come East."

"You've raised it now, it seems."

"Yes; I had a little stroke of luck."

"You're doing well, then?" asked his sister, with a slight show of interest.

If this were so, she was ready to welcome him.

"I said a little show of luck. I got together money enough to come East."

"Oh, indeed!" returned Mrs. Kent, her manner becoming chilly again.

Dick got nettled. He didn't relish his reception.

"It seems to me you ain't very glad to see me," said he, bluntly.

"I never was very demonstrative," said his sister. "Did you expect me to fall on your neck and embrace you?"

"No; but—well, you know what I mean. You are as cold as an icicle."

"It's my way, I suppose. Is your wife living?"

"Yes."

"Is she with you?" asked Mrs. Kent, rather apprehensively.

"No; it was too expensive for me to bring two. I hear you are rich, Helen."

"Is that what brought you on?"

"Don't be so suspicious. It's only natural I should congratulate you."

Before this Nicholas had left the room to go out on his proposed drive.

"I've got enough to live on economically," she answered, with reserve. "I am not rich."

"Your son, Nicholas, acts as if you were."

"How is that?"

Dick laughed.

"He puts on as many heirs as a prince."

"He has considerable spirit," said Mrs. Kent, proudly.

"There's no doubt of that. He ordered me off with the air of a young lord."

"That was before he knew who you were."

"Yes, he didn't know I was his uncle. By the way, you've got a step-son, haven't you?"

"Yes; two-thirds of this property belongs to him."

"Where is he?"

"He is absent just now," answered Mrs. Kent, in a tone of reserve.

Dick laughed.

"Oh, you're good at keeping secrets, Helen," he said; "but you can't deceive me."

"What do you mean?" inquired his sister, with some indignation.

"I know all about his going away, Helen."

"Who told you—the neighbors? Have you been questioning them about my affairs?"

"No, no. You're on the wrong scent this time. He told me himself."

"What! has he got back again?" demanded Mrs. Kent, in surprise and dismay.

"No; I met him in Missouri. He told me there."

"How did he know you were related to me?"

"He heard me and my wife talking about you, and then he told me."

"What did he tell you?"

"That you and he couldn't agree, and so he left home."

"He was insubordinate. He disobeyed me, and I wouldn't stand it."

"Oh, well, you two can settle your own affairs. I don't care to interfere, only I thought you would like to hear from him."

"What's he doing?" asked Mrs. Kent.

"He was in St. Louis when I left, looking out for a situation."

"I wash my hands of him. He might live easily enough if he would submit to me. If not, he will probably have to submit to a great many privations."

"He is a pretty smart boy; he'll get along."

"I consider my Nicholas smarter," said Mrs. Kent, coldly.

"Perhaps so," answered her brother, dubiously. "I don't know much about Nicholas."

"Where are you staying?" asked his sister.

"Why," said Dick, rather taken aback, "I calculated you would invite me to stay here awhile, seeing I've come so far to see you."

Mrs. Kent bit her lips in vexation.

"You can stay a day or two, if you like," she said, "but we live very quietly, Nicholas and I. I don't think it will suit one so active as you are."

"I'll take the risk, sister Helen. It seems good to be in my own sister's house after so many years. Besides, I should like to ride out with my nephew behind that gay horse of his."

"You can speak to him about it," said

Mrs. Kent. "I believe he prefers to be alone."

"Oh, he'll be willing to treat his uncle to a ride. I'll give him a few hints about driving."

Mrs. Kent winced. She was proud, and she did not fancy exhibiting Dick to the village people as her brother. But there seemed no way of avoiding it. She privately determined to get rid of him as soon as possible.

"I must leave you now," she said, gathering up her work. "I will ask the servant to show you your room."

"All right, Helen. Don't trouble yourself about me. I'll make myself at home."

"I'm afraid you will," thought his sister.

CHAPTER XXXIII.

DICK PUNISHES NICHOLAS.

"Is that man going to stay here?" asked Nicholas, in a tone of dissatisfaction.

"Yes."

"What made you invite him?"

"I couldn't help it, Nicholas. He is my brother."

"I'm ashamed of the relationship."

"I am not proud of it myself, but I can't help paying him a little attention."

"How long is he going to stay?"

"A day or two."

"He'll stay a week or two if you let him."

"I can prevent that."

"How?"

"You'll see."

The manner of Nicholas toward his uncle was far from agreeable. In fact, it was almost insolent. Dick retained his temper out of policy, but he said to himself:

"Some time or other, my fine nephew, I'll pay off old scores. See if I don't."

"Are you going to ride this morning?" he asked the next day.

"I may," answered Nicholas.

"I should like to ride with you."

"I prefer riding by myself."

"Oh, come, nephew. I shan't stay here long. Don't refuse such a small favor."

In consequence probably of the first part of this answer, Mrs. Kent said:

"Nicholas, you'd better take your uncle out this morning and show him a little of the village."

Nicholas grumblingly assented.

So about ten o'clock they started out.

"You've got a good horse here," said Dick.

"He ought to be. Mother paid four hundred dollars for him."

"Did she, though? You ought to have got me to send you one from the West. For half the money I'd have sent you a better one."

"I don't believe it."

"Because you don't know. I do."

"It takes a good driver to drive this horse," said Nicholas.

"Does it? I could drive this horse blindfolded."

He spoke contemptuously, and Nicholas was nettled. He prided himself upon his driving ability, and now his uncle underestimated it.

"The horse is not as easy to drive as you think," he said. "If you don't believe it, take the reins and see."

"All right."

This was what Dick wanted, for he had a plan for revenging himself on his upstart nephew. He drove on till he got to a place where there was a muddy and miry puddle beside the road. Then by a dexterous manœuver, for he understood driving thoroughly, he managed to overturn the wagon, and Nicholas was thrown headlong into the puddle. Dick leaped out just at the right time, retaining his hold on the reins.

Bespattered with mud and drenched with mire, Nicholas arose from the puddle a sorry figure.

"What did you do that for?" he demanded, wrathfully, surveying himself with disgust.

"I'm afraid I can't manage your horse," said Dick, with hypocritical meekness. "He was too much for me."

"Didn't I tell you so?" said Nicholas, triumphing in spite of his woful condition.

"I'm sorry you fell into the puddle. Why didn't you jump, as I did?"

"I didn't have time," said Nicholas, ruefully. "What a figure I am!"

"I suppose we may as well go home."

"Yes," said Nicholas, sullenly. "That comes of giving you the reins."

"You are right," said Dick. "You'd better drive home yourself."

Nicholas took the reins, but it mortified him not a little to see the looks of wonder and amusement which he attracted as he passed through the village.

Dick laughed to himself.

"I rather think, my proud nephew, we're about even," he said to himself.

In the course of the next day Dick ventured to suggest to his sister that a temporary loan would be very acceptable.

"A loan!" she repeated, curling her lip. "Why not say 'gift' at once?"

"I'm willing to put it on that ground," said Dick, unabashed. "Still, I'll give you my note for the amount, if you say so."

"What good would that do?"

"Why, I've got some plans in view which, if successful, will enable me to repay you the money, with interest."

"I have small faith in the success of your plans, Richard."

"I haven't been as lucky as you, sister Helen, I admit; but where would you have been but for your lucky marriage?"

"As to that, I have always taken care of myself," said his sister, coldly.

"May be so. There are some born to good luck."

"How much money do you expect me to give you?" asked Mrs. Kent.

Dick looked at his sister's face attentively. He wished to judge how much there was a chance of getting out of her. His survey was not particularly encouraging. She didn't appear to be a woman easily wheedled out of her money. Still, he spoke up boldly, and said:

"A loan of five hundred dollars, Helen, would be a great lift to me."

"I have no doubt it would," said Mrs. Kent, quietly; "but if you have any expectation of getting that sum from me you know very little of me. I should be a fool to throw away such a sum of money."

"You would be generous."

"I have no ambition to be considered generous," she answered, coldly. "A fool and his money are soon parted. You appear to take me for a fool, but I beg to assure you that you are entirely mistaken."

"How much will you lend me, then?" asked Dick, rather sullenly.

"Don't use that ridiculous word 'lend,' when you know there's no probability of your ever repaying it, even if you should be able."

"Have your own way, Helen."

"I will give you fifty dollars, though in justice to my boy I ought not to do so."

"Fifty dollars!" repeated Dick, chagrined. "Why, that don't pay me for coming East."

"You are right. You would have done better to stay where you were."

"You don't seem to consider, Helen, that we hadn't met for years, and I wanted to see my only sister."

"Suppose I had had no money, would you have come then?" asked Mrs. Kent, with contemptuous incredulity.

"No; I couldn't have afforded it. But, Helen, fifty dollars is nothing at all. You might say a hundred."

"I might say a hundred, but there is no chance that I shall. Are you not ashamed—a great, strong man, as you are—not to be able to support yourself and wife without help from me?"

"Luck's been agin me," said Dick, sullenly. "I could have got ahead but for that."

"How has it been against you?"

"I owned a mining claim in California—it didn't pay anything—and I sold it for ten dollars. The man I sold it to kept working till he struck a vein. He cleared ten thousand dollars."

"As you might have done if you hadn't despaired too quickly."

"Oh, well, it's easy enough to criticise, Helen. You've struck a vein, and you're in luck. No more hard work for you."

"There would be if I gave away my money, five hundred dollars at a time. You needn't complain of my good fortune. I have had my share of work to do. Now I am comfortable, and I mean to keep so."

"No matter what becomes of your poor brother?" whined Dick.

"My poor brother must work as I have done, and he won't starve. Do you think, if I were a man," she said, disdainfully, "that I would stoop to ask help of a woman!"

"Well, let me have the money, then," said Dick, gloomily.

Mrs. Kent drew from her pocket-book five ten-dollar bills and placed them in his hand.

"Don't expect any further help," she said. "In justice to my son I must refuse it."

Dick left the house with an execration.

"Was there ever a more selfish, cold-hearted woman?" he muttered. "It's all for her son, is it? I'd like to choke the whelp!"

With this sentiment the affectionate uncle left his sister's house.

CHAPTER XXXIV.

AN IMPORTANT COMMISSION.

It was nearly a year later, and Jasper Kent still remained in St. Louis, and in the employ of Herman Fitch. He had won his way to the favor of his employer, not alone on account of his personal good qualities, but because in the way of business he manifested an unusual aptitude. For this reason he had already had his pay raised to fifteen dollars a week and was thoroughly trusted, even in matters of importance.

Of this he was about to receive an additional proof.

"Jasper," said Mr. Fitch one day, as our hero entered his counting-room, "how would you like a little journey?"

Jasper's eyes brightened.

"I would like nothing better," he answered, promptly.

"So I supposed. Young men of your age generally like to travel."

"To what place do you wish me to go, may I ask, sir?"

"To Kansas—a small town named Plattville."

"Very well, sir, I will go."

"The business is this: A firm in that town, Watts & Duncan, are considerably indebted to me, and I have doubts as their solvency. In the event of their failure I want to realize as much as possible of my claim. I don't want the other creditors to forestall me."

"Yes, sir; I see."

"It is rather a delicate commission, you perceive. You are to go there and quietly find out what you can of their affairs, and report to me by mail. Then I shall send you instructions how to proceed."

"Very well, sir."

"Some might blame me for sending so young a messenger, but I have two objects in view. A boy of your age will not excite suspicion, and again, I repose great confidence in you."

Jasper was not a little gratified by this assurance.

"I will try not to disappoint your expectations," he said, earnestly.

"I don't think you will."

"When do you want me to start?"

"To-morrow."

"I'll be ready," said Jasper, briskly.

"You can go a part of the way by rail, but only a part. It is a frontier town, and you may have to ride horseback a part of the way. That I must leave to your judgment."

"All the better," said Jasper.

"I see you don't mind roughing it," said Mr. Fitch.

"No; that's the best part of it."

"Well, you may go home now and make preparations. To-morrow morning come to the office for instructions and money. One thing only I suggest now—take as little baggage as possible. It would only be in your way."

"All right, sir. I've got a small knapsack that will hold all I want to carry."

"Good! Be here to-morrow at nine o'clock."

At the appointed hour Jasper received his instructions and a certain sum of money. He had provided himself with a belt, into which he put the money to guard against possible robbery, carrying only a few dollars in a pocket-book for outward show.

In explanation of these precautions it must be stated that the events which I am describing took place some years since, when Kansas was more sparsely settled and life less secure than at present.

He received his instructions, and set out on his journey, secretly envied by other clerks who had been longer in the office than himself, but who had not been complimented by having a similar trust reposed in them.

We will follow him and see how he fares.

CHAPTER XXXV.

AN INDIAN MAIDEN.

From the information afforded by his employer Jasper was led to expect a somewhat adventurous journey. He was not to be disappointed. As long as he was in the well-settled part of the country he encountered no difficulties nor adventures worth recording. Plattville, as already stated, was a frontier town, and there was a large tract of almost uninhabited country between it and the nearest settlement.

Late in the afternoon of the fourth day Jasper found himself standing on the bank of a river which must be crossed. There was no boat in sight, and he was puzzled what to do. While he was considering, a young Indian girl glided by in a canoe. She handled the paddle dexterously and as one who had been long accustomed to the exercise, though she did not look more than twelve years of age.

"I wonder if she understands English?" thought Jasper. "Perhaps I could get her to ferry me across."

Acting upon this thought he called out:

"Halloo, there!"

The young girl turned quickly, and discovered Jasper, whom she had not before seen.

She stopped paddling, and asked, in a musical voice:

"White boy speak?"

"Yes," said Jasper. "Do you speak English?"

"A little."

"I want to go across the river. Will you take me in your canoe?"

The girl hesitated a moment, perhaps from uncertainty as to whether she could trust our hero, for she surveyed him attentively. It appeared that her impressions were favorable, for she turned her canoe to the shore and said, simply:

"Yes."

"Thank you," said Jasper, and he promptly took his place in the frail craft.

The Indian girl pushed off and began to paddle rapidly.

"It seems odd to be ferried by a girl," thought Jasper. "I think I ought to offer to take her place." "Shall I paddle instead of you?" he asked.

The girl laughed and shook her head.

"White boy not know how to paddle a canoe—tip it over," and she laughed again.

"I don't know but I should," thought Jasper, as he noticed how light and frail the little canoe was, and how a slight motion would agitate it.

"Do you live around here?" he asked, in some curiosity.

"Up the river," said the girl, indicating with her head, for her hands were occupied.

"Have you a father?"

"Monima's father great chief," said the girl, proudly.

"Monima! Is that your name?"

"Yes."

"It is a pretty name."

The girl laughed and appeared to be pleased with the compliment, though it was only to her name. She seemed in turn to be possessed by curiosity, for she asked:

"What white boy's name?"

"Jasper."

"Jasper," she repeated, with difficulty.

"Isn't it a pretty name?"

"No," said Monima, laughing.

"I am sorry you don't like it, Monima."

"I like white boy. He will be big warrior some day."

"I don't know about that, Monima. So your father is a chief?"

"Yes," said Monima, proudly. "Great chief."

"Did he give you this canoe?"

"Yes."

"Have you any brothers and sisters?"

"One brother, young man; no sister."

By this time they had reached the other side. Monima skilfully drew up the canoe alongside, and Jasper jumped out. He stood on the bank, and drew from his vest-pocket a silver half-dollar, which he handed to Monima.

"Monima no want money," said the girl, proudly.

"Keep it to remember white boy," said Jasper.

"Monima will remember white boy without money."

Jasper reluctantly put the money in his pocket, but he did not like to accept the favor from Monima without rendering her some return. He was in doubt at first, but finally an idea occurred to him. He had half a dozen photographs of himself, which he had recently had taken in St. Louis. He drew out one of these and extended it to Monima.

"Take that, Monima," he said. "Keep that and remember me."

Monima's face lighted up with wonder and admiration when she saw the photograph, for she had never seen one before. She looked from the picture to Jasper, and from Jasper back again to the picture, and laughed softly.

"White boy's picture?" she said.

"Yes, Monima. Do you think it looks like me?"

She nodded emphatically.

"Two white boy—here and there," she said, pointing first to the picture, then to Jasper.

"Good-bye, Monima," he said.

But the Indian girl was evidently tired of the river, for she fastened the canoe and walked by his side. He kept up a conversation for some time, till she turned aside and entered a path which led into the woods.

"Does your father live there?" he asked.

"Yes," said Monima.

"Good-bye," he said.

She didn't say good-bye, but uttered a word which was probably the Indian equivalent for it, and was soon lost to his sight.

"Well, that's romantic, to begin with," thought Jasper. "The daughter of a great chief has ferried me across the river, and I have given her my photograph. The next romantic thing that happens to me may be my losing my way, but I hope not."

He had a general idea of the way he wanted to go, but after awhile he became perplexed, and was led to doubt whether he had not gone astray.

"I wish I could find somebody to guide me," he thought.

He had his wish. A few rods farther on he came upon a man stretched upon the grass under a tree.

"I have lost my way," he began, but before he could finish the sentence the man sprang to his feet, and, to his dismay, he recognized Jack, the man who had had him locked up in St. Louis.

CHAPTER XXXVI.

IN DIFFICULTIES.

Jack looked at first surprised, then smiled with malicious joy as he recognized the boy who accosted him.

"Ha! my chicken, it's you, is it?" he said. "You remember me, don't you?"

"Yes, I remember you," said Jasper.

"I thought I'd get hold of you again some time," said Jack, "but hang me if I expected to find you out here. What brings you here?"

"I came here on business," said Jasper.

"So you are a man of business, are you?" sneered the burglar.

"I am in the employ of Herman Fitch, of St. Louis."

"The father of the boy that Dick kidnapped?"

"Yes."

"Did he send you out here?"

"Yes."

"What for?"

"On a little matter of business," said Jasper, with reserve.

"Oh, that's it. Well, you didn't expect the pleasure of seeing me, did you?"

"I don't consider it a pleasure," said Jasper, boldly.

"Ha! you are a bold boy."

"I speak the truth."

"Well, it isn't always best to speak the truth," said Jack, frowning.

"Shall I lie to you, then?"

"Don't be impudent."

"I shan't say I am glad to see you when I am not."

"Perhaps you are right, boy. You will have no reason to be glad to see me. Follow me."

"I would rather not."

"Follow me, or I will drive this knife into you!" said Jack, savagely, displaying a murderous-looking weapon which he carried in his girdle.

Resistance would have been unavailing and dangerous, and Jasper obeyed, resolved, however, to escape at the first opportunity.

Jack led the way into the woods, not far, however, and finally paused under a large tree.

"Sit down," he said, imperiously.

He threw himself down on the green sward, and Jasper, not very comfortable in mind, sat down near him.

"Now, young fellow," said Jack, "I've got some questions to ask you."

"I suppose he is going to ask me about my escape," thought Jasper, and he was right.

"How did you get away from that room where you were locked up?"

"I got out of the sliding-door," said Jasper.

"How did you get out of the house? Did the old man help you?"

"No," said Jasper.

"Did you go out through the front door?"

"No."

"Don't keep me asking questions," said Jack, harshly. "How did you get out, then?"

"Through the door in the roof. From there I got in through the window into a room in the next house."

"Ha!" said Jack. "I never thought of that. Did you have any trouble with the people there?"

"No; I got into the room of a German, who let me spend the night with him and take breakfast."

"So, that's the way you managed it?"

"Yes."

Jasper felt relieved that no question had been asked him as to Nancy's agency in effecting his release. He would not have betrayed her, at any rate, but his refusal to speak might have incensed Jack.

"Well," he said, "so much for that. Now, how much money have you got with you?"

This was a question which Jasper had expected and dreaded to hear, for nearly all the money in his possession belonged to his employer, and not to himself.

"Well, boy, I want an answer," said Jack, impatiently.

Jasper reluctantly drew out his pocket-book, containing, as we know, but a small portion of his money.

Jack took it, and, opening it, counted the money.

"Only twelve dollars!" he exclaimed, in disgust and disappointment.

"Don't take it," said Jasper, affecting to be very much disturbed.

"What business have you out here with such a paltry sum as twelve dollars?" demanded Jack, angrily.

"That's my business!" said Jasper.

"What do you mean, boy?"

"It certainly isn't your business how much money my employer gave me for expenses."

"Did he expect you to make the whole journey on this contemptible sum?"

"No."

"Where's the rest, then?"

"I am to collect some money before I return," answered Jasper, with a lucky thought.

Jack felt disappointed. The money Jasper was about to collect would do him no good, as, doubtless, the boy would take good care, if once released, not to be caught again.

"That's a miserable way of doing business," said Jack. "Suppose you shouldn't collect it?"

"Then I must write to the firm to send some money."

This gave Jack an idea, on which he afterward acted.

"But," continued Jasper, desirous of getting back some of the money in the pocket-book, "if you take away all my money I can't get to Plattville to make collections."

"Is that where you are to collect money?"

"Yes."

"Will you promise me the money after you have collected it?"

"No," answered Jasper.

"You won't, eh?"

"No; I have no right to. The money won't belong to me."

"That makes no difference."

"It makes a great deal of difference to me."

"Look here, boy," said Jack, frowning, "you evidently don't know the man you're talking to. You ain't going to bluff me off in that way," and he reinforced this declaration with an oath.

"I am trying to be faithful to my employer," said Jasper.

"You've got to be faithful to me."

"What claim have you on me?" asked Jasper.

"You're in my power—that's the claim I have. Do you understand that?"

"I understand what you mean," said Jasper.

"Then I've only to say that it'll be best for you to remember it."

"Tell me again what you want."

"What I did want was, that you should collect this money and bring it to me."

"I refuse."

"You needn't, for I don't intend to let you go out of my sight. I can't trust you. No; I have another plan in view."

Jasper did not ask what it was. He felt sure that it was nothing that he would be willing to do.

"What is the name of your employer?"

"Herman Fitch."

"Very good."

Jack drew from his pocket a small pocket-inkstand, a pen, and some paper.

"Now," said he, "I want you to write a letter."

"Write a letter! To whom?" inquired Jasper, in surprise.

"To this man Fitch, telling him that you have had your pocket picked and need some money. Tell him you will need at least seventy-five dollars, as you haven't been able to collect anything."

"I can't do it," said Jasper.

"Can't do it! What do you mean?"

"I mean that by such a letter I should deceive my employer and be obtaining money from him by false pretenses. I can't do it."

"Look here, boy," said Jack, sternly, "you don't know the man you are trifling with. I am a desperate man, and will stick at nothing. I have taken life before, and I am ready to do so again. Write this letter or I will kill you!"

Jasper listened with horror to this terrible confession and his equally terrible threat.

"Would you take my life for seventy-five dollars?" he said.

"Yes; your life is nothing to me, and I need the money. Quick, your answer!"

As he spoke he drew out a long, murderous-looking knife, and approached Jasper menacingly.

It was a terrible moment. Jack looked as if he fully intended to carry out his threat At any rate, there was danger of it. On the one side was death, on the other breach of trust.

Finally he decided.

"You may kill me if you will," he said at length, "but I won't write the letter."

Jack uttered an execration and raised the knife, but suddenly he uttered a stifled cry and fell to the ground, with blood spurting from a wound in his breast.

Jasper bounded to his feet in astonishment. He had shut his eyes, expecting death. His first glance was at the prostrate brigand. He saw that the wound was made by an arrow, which had penetrated the region of the heart. But who had sped the shaft? And was he also in danger? The question was soon answered.

Out from the underbrush emerged three figures. The foremost was the Indian maiden, Monima. Following her were two men of the same tribe. It was one of these who had shot at Jack.

"Is white boy hurt?" asked Monima, running to Jasper and surveying him anxiously.

"No," said Jasper. "Thank you, Monima."

"Monima is glad," said the Indian girl, joyfully.

Jack groaned, and Jasper came to his side and addressed him compassionately, though but a minute before Jack had been about to take his life. He saw that the blood was gushing forth from his wound.

"Is he badly wounded?" asked Jasper, turning to Monima.

She said something in her native language to the two men.

They spoke briefly, shaking their heads.

"White man will die," she said, interpreting to Jasper.

Our hero was shocked. It was the first time he had ever witnessed a violent death, and it struck him with horror.

He kneeled by Jack's side. Just then the wounded man opened his eyes.

"Who shot me?" he asked, with difficulty.

"The Indians."

Jack's glance fell upon the two men, and he tried to lift himself up, but the effort caused his wound to bleed more copiously. He burst into a volley of oaths, which in his state shocked Jasper.

"Don't swear," he said. "Would you go into the presence of God with an oath in your mouth?"

Jack's face grew livid with terror.

"Who says I am going to die?" he asked, wildly.

"The Indians say you cannot live," said Jasper, gravely.

"It's a lie!" exclaimed Jack, violently. "I'll live to kill you all!"

As he spoke he plucked the arrow from his breast; but this only hastened his death. He fell back exhausted, and in five minutes breathed his last.

Jasper looked so shocked that the Indian girl said, in a tone of surprise:

"Is white boy sorry?"

"Yes," said Jasper.

"What for? He try to kill white boy."

"Yes; but it seems awful to see him killed so suddenly. I wish he could have lived long enough to repent."

Monima could not understand this.

"He bad man!" she said, emphatically. "He try to kill white boy. Monima white boy's friend."

Jasper took the hand of Monima gratefully and said:

"You have saved me, Monima. But for you he would have killed me."

The Indian girl's eyes lighted up, but she only said:

"Monima is glad."

"How fortunate that I fell in with her," thought Jasper, "and that I made a friend of her!"

"Where white boy go to-night?" asked Monima.

"I don't know," said Jasper, doubtfully.

"Come to my father's lodge. In the morning Monima will show the way."

"Thank you, Monima," said our hero. "I will go."

He felt that he could not refuse such an offer from one who had rendered him such a service. Moreover, it relieved him from embarrassment, as he would not have known otherwise where to pass the night, which was now close at hand.

CHAPTER XXXVII.
A STARTLING SUMMONS.

The Indian encampment was only half a mile away. There were assembled about fifty persons, men, women, and children, lying on the grass about the tents. Monima's favor was sufficient to insure a cordial reception to Jasper, who was pressed to partake of supper, an offer he was glad to accept, for it was now seven hours since he had eaten food. After the repast a pipe was offered him, but this he declined, explaining that he never had learned to smoke. On the whole, he enjoyed the adventure, except that he could not help thinking from time to time of his late companion, cut off so suddenly. He learned from Monima that her two attendants had remained behind and buried Jack under the tree where he had been killed.

At night he slept on skins in one of the tents, and in the morning he was guided on his way by Monima as far as the road.

The Indian maiden looked sad when they were about to part.

"When will white boy come back?" she said.

"I don't know, Monima. I hope to see you again, some time, but perhaps you won't remember me."

"Monima never forgets," she answered.

"And I shall not forget."

Attached to his watch was a silver chain which he had bought in St. Louis three months before. He had noticed Momma's look of admiration directed toward it, and he determined to give it to her. Detaching his watch from it, he held it out to the Indian girl.

"Take it, Monima," he said. "It is a gift of friendship."

She uttered a cry of pleasure.

"You give it to Monima?" she said, half incredulous.

"Yes," he said.

"And I have nothing to give white boy," she said, sadly.

"You have given me my life. Is that nothing, Monima? Keep the chain, and whenever you look at it remember Jasper."

So they parted, and Jasper pursued his journey to Plattville. He reached the town without further adventure, and conducted satisfactorily the business with which he was intrusted. He succeeded in obtaining half the money due his employer, and in making arrangements for the speedy payment of the rest. So it was with a mind well satisfied that he returned to St. Louis.

When he told Mr. Fitch the particulars of his encounter with Jack, and his escape, the latter said, earnestly:

"Jasper, you are the bravest boy I know."

"I am afraid you overrate my services," said Jasper, modestly.

"And you really refused to write the letter, though you knew your life was in danger?"

"I was not willing to betray my trust."

"I honor your courage and fidelity, but you carried them too far. We would far rather have lost ten times seventy-five dollars than risked your life."

"I didn't think of that, I only thought it would be wrong to defraud you."

"We shall not forget your fidelity. You may consider your wages raised to twenty dollars a week."

"Thank you, sir," said Jasper, gratified.

"It is not merely on account of your courage and fidelity, but partly because of the business ability you have shown in carrying on this affair."

Again Jasper thanked his employer, and went about his duties with fresh courage, feeling that his services were appreciated.

"I am glad I came to St. Louis," he thought. "How much better I am situated than I should have been at home, tyrannized over by a step-mother by whom I was disliked."

Three months more passed, when one day a boy entered the store.

"Is Jasper Kent here?" he asked.

"Yes," said Jasper, coming forward, "that is my name."

"I have a telegram for you," said the boy. Jasper tore it open, and read these words:

"Come home at once. Your step-mother is dying.

"OTIS MILLER."

Shocked at this startling intelligence, Jasper at once sought his employer, obtained leave of absence, and took the next train bound east.

We must precede him and explain what had happened, and what occasioned Mrs. Kent's critical condition.

CHAPTER XXXVIII.

DICK COMES BACK.

When Mrs. Kent's brother left her house with fifty dollars in his pocket she warned him that it was the last money he could expect to receive from her. He did not reply, but he had no intention of remaining satisfied with so little.

"What is fifty dollars?" he thought, "to my sister's fortune? She needn't think she has got rid of me so easily."

At that time he expected to make her another visit in the course of a month or two, but circumstances prevented. The fact is, he was imprudent enough to commit theft and incautious enough to be detected, not long afterward, and the consequence was a term of imprisonment.

When he was released from confinement he at once made his way to his sister's house.

As before, Nicholas was standing on the lawn. His countenance changed when he recognized his uncle, though he didn't know that he had just come from a prison.

"How are you, Nicholas?" said his uncle.

"I'm well," said his nephew, coldly.

"Really, you have grown a good deal since I saw you."

Even this compliment did not soften Nicholas, who turned his back and did not invite his uncle into the house.

Dick scowled in an ugly manner but controlled his voice.

"How is your mother?"

"She's got the headache."

"I am sorry. I have been sick, too."

Nicholas did not exhibit the slightest curiosity on the subject.

"I have just come from the hospital," a slight fiction, as we know.

This aroused Nicholas, who retreated a little as he asked:

"Did you have anything catching?"

"No; besides, I'm well now. I should like to see your mother."

"I don't think she feels well enough to see you."

"Will you go up and see? I want to see her on important business."

Nicholas went up stairs grumbling.

"Well, mother," he said, "that disreputable brother of yours has come again."

Mrs. Kent's brow contracted.

"Where is he?" she asked.

"Down stairs. He wants to see you, he says."

"How does he look?"

"Worse than ever. He says he has just come from a hospital."

"From a hospital? He has a good deal of assurance to come here," said Mrs. Kent, with a hard look.

"So he has."

"I will tell you why," said his mother, in a lower tone. "He has not told you the truth. He has not come from a hospital, as he represents."

"Why should he say so, then?" asked Nicholas, surprised.

"Because he didn't like to say prison."

"Has he been in prison? How do you know?"

"I saw an account in the papers of his arrest and conviction. I suppose he has just come out of prison."

"Why didn't you tell me of this before, mother?"

"I wanted to keep the disgrace secret, on account of the relationship. When he finds I know it, I shall soon be rid of him."

"Will you see him, then?"

"Yes; I will go down stairs, and you may tell him to come in."

Two minutes later the ex-convict entered his sister's presence. He read no welcome in her face.

"Hang it!" he said, "you don't seem very glad to see your only brother."

"You are right," she said; "I do not seem glad, and I do not feel glad."

His face darkened as he sank heavily into an arm-chair.

"I suppose I'm a poor relation," he said, bitterly. "That's the reason, isn't it?"

"No."

"You'd treat me better if I came here rich and prosperous."

"Probably I would."

"Didn't I say so? You haven't any feelings for the poor."

"I haven't any feeling for criminals," said Mrs. Kent, in a sharp voice.

He uttered a stifled oath and his face flushed.

"What do you mean?" he asked.

"I mean that you came here straight from a prison; deny it if you can," she said, sternly.

He hesitated. Then he said:

"I'm not the only innocent man that's been locked up."

"You can't deceive me," she answered, "though you protest your innocence all day. I shall not believe you. I feel sure that you were guilty of the crime for which you were punished."

"It's rather hard that my own flesh and blood should turn against me."

"You have disgraced the family," said Mrs. Kent. "I discard you. I no longer look upon you as my brother."

"If you had not turned me off with such a pittance it wouldn't have happened," he said, sullenly. "Out of your abundance you only gave me fifty dollars."

"And you a stout, broad-shouldered man, must accept charity or steal!" she said, sarcastically.

"Luck has always been against me."

"Your own bad habits have always been against you."

"Look here," said he, doggedly, "I won't stand any more of that, even from my own sister."

"Very well. What have you come here for?"

"I'm out of money."

"And you expect me to supply you?"

"I think you might give me a little, just to get along."

"I shall not give you a cent. You have no claim upon me. I have already said that I no longer look upon you as a brother."

"Is that all you've got to say?" demanded Dick, his face growing dark with anger.

"It is my final determination."

"Then all I've got to say is, you'll repent it to the last day of your life!" he burst out, furiously. "I'll go away"—here he arose—"but I'll never forget your cruelty and harshness."

He strode out of the room, and she looked after him coldly.

"It is as well," she said to herself. "Now he understands that there is no more to be got out of me, I hope I shall never lay eyes upon him again."

"Well," said Nicholas, entering directly afterward, "what have you said to him? He dashed out of the yard, looking as black as a thunder-cloud."

"I told him that he had disgraced the family and I should never more acknowledge him as a brother."

"I'm glad you sent him off with a flea in his ear. I don't want to see him around here again."

"I don't think we shall."

There was one thing Mrs. Kent forgot—her brother's brutal temper and appetite for revenge. Had she thought of this she would, perhaps, have been more cautious about provoking him.

In the middle of the night Mrs. Kent awoke with a strange sense of oppression, the cause of which she did not immediately understand. As soon as she recovered her senses she comprehended the occasion—the crackling flames—and the fearful thought burst upon her:

"The house is on fire!"

She threw on her dress and dashed hastily from the room. She was about to seek the quickest mode of exit when she thought of Nicholas. He might be asleep, unconscious of his peril. She was a cold and selfish woman, but her one redeeming trait was her affection for her son. She rushed frantically to his chamber, screaming:

"Nicholas! Wake up! The house is on fire!"

She entered his chamber, but he was not in it. He had already escaped, and, full of selfish thoughts of his own safety, had fled without giving heed to his mother, though there would have been time for him to save her.

"He is safe!" thought Mrs. Kent, and, relieved of this anxiety, she sought to escape.

But the flames had gained too much headway. Her dress caught fire, and she ran frantically about, ignorant that in so doing she increased the peril. She was barely conscious of being seized and borne out by friendly hands. But though the flames were extinguished, she had already received fatal injuries. She lingered till the afternoon of the following day, and then died. Meanwhile Mr. Miller sent Jasper the telegram already referred to.

Nicholas looked serious when he was informed of his mother's death, but his was not a temperament to be seriously affected by the misfortune of another. His own interests were uppermost in his mind.

"Will I get mother's property?" he asked Mr. Miller, while that mother lay dead and disfigured in his presence.

"This is no time to speak of property," said Mr. Miller, coldly. "You ought to think of your poor mother's fate."

"Of course I do," said Nicholas, trying to look sorrowful; "but I want to know how I'm going to be situated."

"Wait till after the funeral, at any rate," said the other, disgusted.

CHAPTER XXXIX.

HOW IT ALL ENDED.

Jasper did not reach home till after the funeral had taken place and his step-mother was buried. Though he had little reason to like her, he was shocked and distressed by her sad and untimely fate.

"How could the house catch fire, Mr. Miller?" he asked.

"It is supposed to have been set on fire."

"Who would do it?"

"From what Nicholas tells me I suspect that the fire was the work of Mrs. Kent's brother."

"Her brother!" exclaimed Jasper. "I met him in the West."

"Then you probably know that he was not a very respectable character."

"I know that he was concerned in kidnapping a child."

"Nicholas tells me that he had just got out of prison, and applied to Mrs. Kent for help, which she refused. Incensed at this, he probably set the house on fire."

"I think he would be capable of doing it. Has he been arrested?"

"Not yet, but the police are on his track. I don't think he can escape."

"Nicholas doesn't seem to take his mother's death very hard."

"No. I am disgusted with his selfishness. He seems to be principally concerned about property which she leaves."

"I suppose he will inherit it."

"Yes. I don't know in what state it is, but it ought to amount to thirty thousand dollars. It is a large slice of your father's fortune."

"I do not begrudge it to him. I shall have enough."

"That reminds me that it is time to open the instrument which your father left with me."

The paper was opened then and there, and proved to contain the following direction: That in case Jasper and his step-mother did not get along harmoniously, his old friend, Mr. Miller, was empowered and requested to assume the guardianship of Jasper.

"That arrangement suits me precisely," said Jasper, warmly. "Will you accept the trust?"

"Cheerfully," said his friend. "I don't think there is any danger of our disagreeing."

Jasper shook his head.

"If there should be any disagreement it would be my fault," he said. "But won't Nicholas need a guardian?"

"Yes; one will have to be appointed."

"I suppose his uncle would be willing to take the post."

"His uncle, if found, will hardly be in a position to act in that capacity."

Dick was not found. He disappeared, and from that day was not seen in the neighborhood. It is supposed that he went West and found a secure concealment in some of the distant territories, where probably he is engaged in the same discreditable courses for which he was already notorious.

As was anticipated, Nicholas inherited about thirty thousand dollars. He selected as his guardian the young physician whom his mother had employed in her husband's last sickness. But the man proved faithless to his trust, and ran away with the entire fortune of his ward, leaving him absolutely penniless.

In this emergency Nicholas, humbled and mortified, appealed to Jasper to help him.

With his guardian's permission, Jasper agreed, during his good behavior, to pay for his use an annual sum of five hundred dollars, urging him to continue at school. But this did not suit Nicholas. He obtained a place in New York, where he soon developed fast tendencies, and ended by running away with a considerable sum of money belonging to his employer. It was believed that he went to California. His employer took no steps to apprehend him, Jasper having agreed to make up to him the sum—nine hundred dollars—which Nicholas had appropriated. For him it was a saving, since by his conduct Nicholas had forfeited the annual provision he had agreed to make for him.

And what became of Jasper? By his guardian's advice he went to school for two years more. Then he returned to St. Louis, and again entered the employment of Mr. Fitch.

At twenty-one, with a portion of his property, he bought an interest in the business and became junior partner, and is now one of the most respected and enterprising young business men in that flourishing city. He was recently united in marriage to a charming young lady, the daughter of a prosperous Western merchant, and so his prospects seem as bright as could well be hoped for.

The trials of his early life are safely passed.

By his honesty, courage and generosity he has fairly earned the happiness which he enjoys. Nor has he forgotten Nancy and the Indian maiden who rendered him so essential a service at a critical point in his fortunes. Every year he sends them a handsome present, choosing the articles which are best suited to gratify their tastes.

Monima cherishes a romantic attachment for her benefactor, and will not soon forget the "white boy," whose picture she carries with her in all her wanderings.